BREWED ANEW

DARLENE EVERLY

Hardcover: ISBN 978-1-954719-44-6

Paperback: ISBN 978-1-954719-43-9

Ebook: ISBN 978-1-954719-42-2

First paperback edition August 2022.

Edited by Jupiter Alley.

Cover art by Jupiter Alley.

Layout by Wishing Well Books.

WA, US

DARLENE EVERLY

Brewed Anew

A COMFORT FOOD ROMANCE

Personal Pan and Cupcake Queens were just the beginning of the Comfort Food romances, now here's Brewed Anew! If you would like to be the first to hear about the next book in the series titled Favorite Beans, get free books and an exclusive short story in this series, as well as see what else the author has written, please go to darleneeverly.com and sign up for her newsletter.

Happily Ever Brewing!

For the distances that don't matter
And the ones that keep

MARCUS

Some things were just too cute.

The Mason Jar Brewery was one of them.

At some point, I needed to remember to ask Vanessa if the idea for the name and all the corresponding things—like the Mason jar beer steins—was her idea. Because if it was, she was a genius. Of course, I was biased.

But, for now, all I could do was wander through the tasting room, and try to familiarize myself with the space.

"I mean, these tables..."

Running my hand along the top of one of the long, picnic-style, farmhouse tables, I marveled at the surprisingly soft, smooth feel of the finish. They looked like they would be rough.

Along the center of the table, small stands of clear plastic held the menu for the beer, and more paper menus were placed at regular intervals along both sides.

Hmmm...It seemed like there was so much more we could do with the menus, the center of the table, and the place itself.

It was all adorable, like a covered carpentry shop from someone's Pinterest board of historic barn weddings. There were even some details I recognized from a friend's board for their own wedding last year.

Part of me assumed that my friend had included me in all her digital brainstorming for her day because she thought her gay friend would automatically have good taste.

Being gay didn't give me good taste. I knew lots of gay and straight people with zero taste. Being me gave me good taste.

Although, according to Ceecee, that only applied to anything having to do with marketing and decorating. She didn't think I should be allowed to dress myself, or pick out menu items.

Ceecee was a brat, and I only put up with her thinking so little of me because I loved her completely.

I smiled at the thought of telling her all about this place as I straightened some menus and wandered to the giant bar.

Now this bar... there was nothing I would change.

Well-stocked, the kegs of each brew were in what looked like old whiskey barrels. But I knew they were state-of-the-art new on the inside, so the taste wouldn't be changed.

"Marcus," Vanessa said, coming behind the bar, and smiling at me, "what do you think?"

She tapped the leather-finished, granite top near the order station. "Do you think you can make this tasting room work better than it does?"

"You know," I said, leaning against the counter behind me where all the glassware sat in its neat, sparkling rows above and below on the live edge shelves, "I have a few thoughts, but I really want to work in the space for a week or so before I suggest anything."

"Perfect," she said, with a bounce, her voice energized, "that way you can have time to work with Andrew, too, and really get to know all the ways we can make this brewery better."

Her grin was massive, but the same thing happened to me when she had offered me the job. I wondered if there was more riding on my ability to come up with some kind of marketing change to improve the business than she let on.

What it was, I had no idea. The business was successful, turning a healthy profit, and had been since its inception two years ago—enough to warrant this location and the other location in California.

So, leveling up made sense. But she was so eager...I set it aside, deciding I was being paranoid after what Ceecee just went through.

"When will I meet Andrew?" I asked, opening the little cupboards beneath the bar, and checking on all the supplies inside.

"He should be here soon. I know he wanted to be here for the last two weeks. But he has a lot going on, and was out of town."

Just like the last few times she mentioned her business partner, her answers told me nothing about the man. But some people were very private about certain aspects of their lives.

If it was something like a death in the family that pulled him away, I understood not wanting to say anything.

As much as I actually did understand, it was still almost impossible to keep my mouth shut.

"What did you think about the cicerone class you took?" she asked with a grin on her face.

"Oof." I shook my head, and she laughed.

"That was a lot, I know," she said, perching on one of the bar stools.

"For you, I'm sure it was a breeze. Beer is what you do. But for me, it was like being thrown into the deep end of a pool filled with hops, and not knowing how to swim."

Her laugh was freer this time, and seemed at home next to the bar. There was a wild edge to it that made me think it would carry over the sounds of a room full of people enjoying themselves.

One day, I hoped I had a laugh that powerful.

She wiped the corners of her eyes, and managed to get her laughter back under control with a contrite smile on her face.

"I really am sorry, but there was no better way to prepare you for working here. It would have been worse if we just started you in the tasting room without any idea what you were talking about, or how to discuss the flavors."

"Vanessa," I leaned on the bar toward her, and smiled back. Maybe if I was relaxed when I said this, she would finally believe me that, even though it was tough, it was fine. "I've been around enough foodies to know how helpful those classes were."

"Good." She let out a heavy breath, as if bracing for me to say something different than I had already explained on the phone. "But I needed to hear it from you in person."

"Have all the employees gone through the classes?" I asked, wondering at the expense of that.

"Not all of them, but most. And some have even gone back and taken it a second time after working here for long enough to really understand it all. The ones who do that become certified cicerones."

"Amazing." I shook my head, stood up, and looked out over the tasting room, trying and failing to do the math in my head. "Does that make this the most qualified brewery around?"

"Believe it or not, I have no idea." She laughed again, and hopped down off the stool, patting a hand on the bar. "But I know we must have some of the best and most dedicated staff around. It's how we've done so well so fast."

"I think it may also have something to do with being good at actually brewing tasty beer." I gestured to the kegs around me, and she nodded.

"Yes, but there are a lot of places that make a decent beer, and a lot that make a damn good beer. There has to be something special about this place, don't you think?"

"Of course," I said, and smiled, even though we were back to the hard sell that struck me as odd. I just wasn't sure how else to react.

The door to the brewery itself banged open, and a jean-clad leg stuck out into the tasting room, holding the door open.

"Vanessa, are you in here?" called a deep voice that sounded vaguely familiar from the other side of the door.

"Andrew?" she asked, hustling toward him, me trailing behind.

"Come help me with this," he said.

She reached him, and held the door open as he walked in backward, rolling in a keg, before I even got to that end of the room.

"I'm glad you're here early," Vanessa said to him, and looked past him to smile at me, "you have time to meet our new front of house."

"Van, we talked about this. You were supposed to wait until I got back to hire someone."

Wait…he didn't know she hired me?

Few times in my life I had wanted to find a table to hide under more than right at that moment. If she hadn't told him, would he want to fire me?

"Andrew," she said, plastering a wide-eyed, forced smile on her face, "meet Marcus Mason."

He stiffened and stood up straight, making me swallow and do the same.

I could have sworn I saw the small, dark hairs along the deep, brown skin of his neck stand on end.

This was bad.

She didn't tell him, and he didn't want me here. Clearly, I needed to leave.

"You know, maybe I can just…" I gestured over my shoulder toward the door to the parking lot, and took a step back.

But it was too late.

Andrew turned toward me, a close-cropped beard coming into view along with dark, brown eyes that I knew.

"Shane," I said, my voice hushed as the pain of a thousand days flashed through my mind, and I stared into the warm eyes I dreamed about long after he left me with no explanation.

"Marcus," my ex-boyfriend said, his voice devoid of all emotion.

SHANE

When I left California this time, I thought my biggest challenges of the whole trip home would be telling Vanessa I still didn't know how I would do what she needed me to, and coming up with a way to make it happen.

Getting up this morning, I thought the biggest challenge of today would be having the tough conversations I needed to have with Van before she headed to her own home for a while.

The last thing I expected was to have my life flash before my eyes before lunch time.

Of course, it wasn't my life. Not the one I was leading, and not even the one I led back when Marcus and I were together.

"Andrew," Van said, her voice holding a forced cheerfulness that made me feel bad for a second, "meet Marcus Mason."

Everything stopped.

For the rest of the world, the Earth continued to spin, the universe continued to move, and their lives probably didn't change at this exact second of this exact day the way mine did with her words.

Somehow, no matter how ridiculous the excuses running

through my mind, I couldn't believe it was him. Not at first. Not really.

All I could do was think that someone else must have had the same name. Someone else must have had the same perfect, terrible name that haunted me all the time in ways that I invited, and ways that I wished would stop.

But once I turned around and saw him, my brain stuttered to a halt, and it couldn't continue to drum up anything false.

Marcus was too true.

No, it wasn't a life lived by me or anyone else that flashed by me in that moment. It was the life I thought we would live together.

Marcus with his hair mussed in the morning, wearing those hideous, old t-shirts he collected from high school sports competitions that he preferred to wear for pajamas, and making coffee with too much sugar in it.

Soft, morning light would be starting to filter through the large windows of the little one-bedroom apartment we dreamed about at the time with our modest, college budgets. It would shine on him, illuminating the work of art he was, transforming that little turn of the corner of his lips that he reserved for just me into an angelic gift of a smile.

Every minute of every day since I left him with nothing but a stupid letter tucked into the book he was reading that sat on the nightstand, I thought about all the things I missed and desperately wished to have back.

Being with Marcus was more than some crush between high school sweethearts away at college together. Having him in my life, knowing he was there for me, was like armor against all the possible ills of the world.

More than just the mornings were better because he was in them.

I missed him every second since I left, since I begged

everyone that we knew not to tell him where I went or any of the few details that I shared with them.

They understood. They knew as well as I did that if he knew the real reason that I was leaving, he would have dropped everything, and given up his entire life to help me. There was no way I could do that to him.

I loved him too much.

As soon as Van said his name, it was as if I was back there, in one of the worst moments of my life.

I stood in his dorm room after he left for school. I let myself in with the key he had made for me, and the letter in the other hand. I treasured that key.

We kissed in the doorway of his room the night before, right before I went back to my own dorm so he could study for his test in the morning, and right before I would get the world's worst phone call.

But even though I spent all night long awake, crying, agonizing, and crafting that letter along with messages to all our friends, my hand still stalled on the way to the nightstand.

Putting that letter in his book so it wouldn't fall down with a gust of wind like his birthday card did would be the final step. It would be goodbye.

A perfunctory letter that didn't tell him what it should have.

Finally, my vision blurred with tears I wouldn't let fall. I shoved the letter in the book, and ran from the room that held too many memories and too much hope.

Running into walls on the way out, I leaned against the back of the elevator, not hearing the sound of it moving, or the sounds of the people around me even after the doors slid open again.

The dorm was never really empty, even at that moment when most classes were in session, but I didn't notice the faces of the people that I passed as I stumbled my way out to my packed car.

Only once I was all the way outside, and safely inside my car did I break.

Sobs, the same kind that ripped through me on and off all night long while I made arrangements and packed, tore me apart all over again.

For a year afterward, those same sobs would be my almost-nightly companions. It got to the point where I kind of missed them once my eyes finally dried up.

Now, though, my chest constricted, and the old memory of them built inside me even as I tried to remember that Marcus wasn't my Marcus anymore.

How could he be?

After all I did, after all we lost, there was no way he wanted to see my tears. It wouldn't be fair of me to subject him to them.

Instead, I tried to accept whatever I would hear next. I tried to listen, tried to be willing to hear about his boyfriend, his fiancé, his husband.

Because a guy like Marcus, one who loved with everything in him, funny, kind, with a cheeky smile and soft eyes had to be wanted by everyone.

The few friends I kept in contact with from back then never gave me updates about Marcus. Then again, I never asked.

Maybe Tommy, our old friend who always had a crush on Marcus, swooped in to pick up the pieces I left behind of the shattered life Marcus and I had planned.

No matter who he was with now, no matter what his life had become, it took a desperate effort for me not to reach out and grab Marcus. For me not to pull him into a hug, not to breathe him in until I felt his heart beating against mine, and the comforting wash of his breath as he fit into my arms the way he always had before...I couldn't. None of those things were mine to do.

All I could do now was pretend to be comfortable to make

sure he stayed, make sure he was here for as long as I could keep him here.

Our life, our plans were all gone and over, but if he worked here, I could see him every day. And that was more than I ever thought I would have again.

"Who's Shane?" Vanessa asked, looking back and forth between us.

"Um," he said, rubbing a hand over the back of his neck, and shaking his head as he looked away from me. "I am. Or, I was."

I took a deep, shuddering breath, and curled my hands into fists at my sides.

"That's what everyone called him in school because there were too many Andrews," I said, trying to keep my voice as cold as I wanted it to be. He didn't deserve to get any more of my emotions.

"But that doesn't make any sense." She still looked back and forth like she was watching a tennis match. At some other time, I probably would have thought it was funny.

I didn't find anything in this to laugh about.

"My friends picked the name Shane from my last name," he said, and shrugged.

Shrugged. As if coming face to face with me, as his employee—of all the ridiculous ways—was just another day at the brewery.

"They turned Shanterly into Shane? Wow, that seems like a leap."

Oh, good. They were chuckling. This was all a big joke to them. Look what happened when the new guy showed up to work.

While they discussed all the ways in which childhood nicknames were odd, and how small a world this was for me to arrive here, I was trying to calculate how long I could live off my savings if I walked out before they got back to noticing I was there.

Not long enough.

"You moved," I said, stupidly, not hearing what they said before they both turned their eyes to me.

"I…no. Not really. Only for a while," Shane said.

Right. So that was a lie. One that all the people we knew told me.

This was so much worse than I was ever aware of. And that was bad enough.

A pressure built in the back of my brain. I was seconds away from screaming.

"Well," Vanessa said, smiling as if my head wasn't going to explode, "since you two know each other, this should go even better than I thought. Marcus is going to start in here today as mostly an observer and helper. Can you help him get his legs under himself this week?"

She turned to Shane, who barely glanced at me, and nodded, his jaw tight.

"But for now," I said, interrupting whatever they were about to discuss next. "I need to step out for…" forever, "a minute."

Vanessa opened her mouth like she was going to say something, but Shane shook his head at her as I passed.

I walked through the nearest door, just to get away from them that much faster.

Unfortunately, I walked into the kitchen.

Where was the door to the parking lot?

Making my way through the kitchen, opening each of the doors I came to. I knew it was here. I actually knew where it was. But my mind was mush. And I had to get out.

Right now. Before my shaking legs gave out under me.

Finally, I swung the door open to the parking lot, and stepped out into the gray morning, dragging in breaths of the chilled air.

With fingers that didn't want to work properly, I fumbled in my pocket for my keys and my phone, dropping the keys to the gravel below me in the process.

Swearing under my breath, I bent forward to collect them. The door behind me swung open, and the light from the kitchen glinted off the metal of my keys.

He cleared his throat, and I snapped up, a wave of dizziness accompanying the sudden movement. But I gritted my teeth, refusing to fall over.

Not in front of Shane. Not now.

"Marcus," he said, and in his voice was the same sad tone I heard before in his last message when he left without telling me why.

I shook my head, and walked toward my car on legs that were too stiff just to keep me upright.

Getting my finger to hit the right button on the key fob was a lesson in sheer determination, but I did it.

And I flung the car door open before collapsing inside, then slammed it behind me.

Shane stood in the open doorway to the kitchen, looking like he was doing nothing more than waiting for a bus.

Making my hands work to call Ceecee was easy. At least in that, the need to protect myself, to have her help, overrode whatever weakness was happening with my body.

"Come on. Come on," I mumbled to the empty car while Shane watched me.

Finally, she picked up, her voice all sunshine and light since she just got her girlfriend back.

"Marcus, I thought you were at work," she said. The sound of one of her timers being set dinged in the background.

"I…" Oh, god. Tears threatened at the backs of my eyes.

"Hey, Honey, what's wrong?"

"Shane…" I couldn't get out the words. Nothing wanted to come out of my throat in anything that resembled a sentence, not while I sucked down breath after breath, and not enough air was getting into my body.

"What? Marcus? What's going on?"

"Ceecee, Shane is here." I was in a nightmare. This wasn't real. It was the only explanation. But Shane still stood in the doorway, staring at me.

"What? Why the hell is Shane back? Did he say anything? And why is he at your work?" Her voice had gone from cheer, to concern, to panic, to fury.

She was traversing the whole scope of human emotions while I still didn't know how to get past this blank, shaking, generally ill feeling to land on anything close to what she was expressing. But my head felt like it was all building into a volcano buried in me, and I wasn't sure what would happen when it finally exploded.

"He's the co-owner," I said into the phone, choosing to tell her the one thing I knew for sure. Of all the things running through my head and slamming into my skull freezing me in place, the one true thing I knew was that.

Ceecee sucked in a breath, and the other end of the phone went silent.

I pulled the phone away from my ear, and looked at the screen. The call was still connected.

"Um," I said, not sure what else there was.

"Sorry, I think I blacked out for a minute. Did you say he's the co-owner? How is that possible?"

After a quick rundown of the situation—through which she kept making a noise somewhere between a scoff and an incredulous snort of humorless laughter—we sat in silence.

Picturing Ceecee with her mouth hanging open, trying to find the words, all I could say was, "Yeah."

"Listen, Marcus, this doesn't mean anything," she said.

"How can you say that? You were there. Through all the tears. You know."

Just remembering the time I spent, the mess I was, it made my throat close up.

"Yes, I do know. Which is why I'm telling you, you are not the same guy he left behind. You are a grown man. And you are excited about this job and this work. They're giving you the chance to do all kinds of things. Don't let his presence take those things from you the way he took so much from you by being absent."

Ceecee was brilliant. And mean.

"Fine. But when there are tears—and you know there will be —I'm going to blame you and make you wipe them off my face."

"Better. Hang on…"

Sounds of her talking with someone coupled with muffled swear words made me wonder if something got burnt while she ignored her baking to talk to me.

"Marcus?" Theresa, Ceecee's girlfriend asked on the other end of the phone.

"Hi, Theresa." Great. My little break down was a whole family affair.

"You know I have access to heavy digging equipment and concrete," she said.

I laughed.

She managed to make me burst out laughing, although I wouldn't have believed someone if they told me I was capable of it a few minutes ago.

"Today you'll be open to customers, and in the front, right?" she asked.

"The brewery will be…" Even with Ceecee's pep talk, how was I going to make it through an entire day with Shane around, let alone all the ones after?

"Good, and so will you, and everyone we know."

More muffled sounds as I pulled the phone away from my face to look at the screen. That didn't make sense.

"Theresa?"

"No, I'm back," Ceecee said. "She's making calls."

"What is she doing? I don't actually want him dead." I mean…I probably didn't. No, I definitely didn't. Too many questions.

"She's not going to kill him. Yet."

I grinned and rubbed a hand over my face.

"But I'm not making any promises for everyone else if he's terrible to you," she said.

"Everyone else?" Who was she including in that?

"We're working it out now. Some of them are babies."

"Hey," Theresa yelled in the background.

"Tee, you're *my* baby, but you're twenty. Still a baby."

"Ceecee, focus." What were they talking about?

I was having an emotional breakdown, and they were yammering about their age difference? It wasn't even that much. What on Earth?

"Marcus, it's a brewery. You can't have all your twenty-year-old friends show up, and get you in trouble."

"Wait, you're coming here?" My voice cracked on 'here.' And who all was she including in the list of my twenty-year-old friends?

"Of course I am. Deacon already had his birthday. Campbell is old enough. Deacon is recruiting teammates, and Katie is bringing who knows how many people."

"How?" It had only been seconds. How did that happen so fast?

"Group text. Theresa knows good people."

"I know that, but..." But what? My friends, people who mostly just adopted me out of my proximity to Ceecee, were dropping everything to be here for me?

All the pressure of wanting to cry rushed into the backs of my eyes again.

"No buts. If Shane thinks he is going to get a replay of the way he ditched you last time, and took all but one of your friends with him, he's sorely mistaken."

"Yeah." I got the better end out of that deal.

I shook my head in wonder at Ceecee and Theresa and all their friends.

"Hey," Theresa said on the phone now, "Deacon wants to know how many boyfriends you want."

"Wait, what?" I choked on nothing, leaving me with a hacking laugh.

"Deacon says that he and the other guys from the team are more than willing to stand in as your boyfriend or boyfriends for the day."

"Boyfriends?"

"Yeah, he says they're signing up with like a schedule, so you won't be without some backup all day."

Multiple fake boyfriends all from the university's football team?

I was on Earth Two. It was the only explanation.

"And Katie is bringing like half of Greek row."

"Half of..." Was there even enough beer for all the college kids who were going to crowd into the tasting room? Were there enough servers? "Maybe this is getting a little out of hand."

"Nope. We're doing this. And they want your work schedule."

"Come on, Theresa, we can't have the entire UW in the

brewery today. That would be a little suspicious, don't you think?"

"See you later, Marcus," Ceecee said, and they hung up.

I looked at the phone, brought it back to my ear, and said, "Hello?" even though I knew they hung up.

"What in the world?" I didn't know what they were about to unleash here. I wasn't sure if I wanted it, or how much of a mess this would turn into.

But I swallowed, and dropped the phone into my lap knowing I was along for the ride now, no matter what I thought.

And I couldn't think. Not really.

The only thing I could do for the next moment was look at the steering wheel in front of me while being aware of the figure in my peripheral vision of Shane still standing in the doorway and looking my way.

SHANE

"What are you doing?" Van asked, her voice quiet as she came up behind me.

"Looking." Yes, that was true. All I did was look. Look at who I lost, look at who I was shocked I was able to even see again. And I had no idea how to explain it all to her.

"What are you looking at?" Her voice was even more hushed than before, as if she could feel how off I was, and was afraid to disturb me enough to cause the tears trapped inside me to flow down my face.

"Him." How could so much be summed up in such a simple word? I was looking at him, and everything that I wrapped up along with him in my deep well of pain.

"Andrew, please." She sounded exasperated, but I still couldn't turn to look at her. I couldn't take my eyes from him. "Tell me what's going on."

"Remember when I first got to California and cried a lot?" I asked, my throat tight as Marcus tilted his head back, and leaned against the headrest of the seat in his car.

"Of course. You had a lot to deal with." She placed a featherlight palm on my shoulder blade, and it was everything I could do to keep it together.

"Part of what I was dealing with was leaving Marcus."

"You…" She sucked in a noisy breath, and I squeezed my eyes shut for a second to keep the tears back. "He's your ex? He's the Mason guy that you…"

I opened my eyes again, and didn't trust myself to speak. So, I simply nodded.

"But you said he didn't want to come with you, to do what you had to do. You said he had a life he wanted to lead, and that didn't include leaving here."

From the kitchen behind me, warm air pressed against me, and from the front the chill of the wet day.

Everything about today was two-at-once, including seeing Marcus, looking at him now. It was both pain and joy.

I needed to tell her, no matter how much it would make the pain take over.

"He did have a life here, and things he wanted to do. We talked about all of them. But I made the choice for him. I didn't even tell him where I was going or why because I knew he would destroy himself to help me."

That supportive palm on my back became a hard shove.

"Are you kidding me? That's the stupidest thing I've ever heard, Andrew."

"Van, I know, okay? I've known for a long time. But there's not a damn thing I can do about it now, and there wasn't the second I did it. He would never be okay with what I did. I'm not, so how could he be?" I shook my head, crossing my arms tight across my chest, and taking a deep, shuddering breath.

"Do you think he's going to quit?" she asked, her voice hard enough that I heard the unspoken part of her question. Did I think she needed to stay here longer?

"You don't have to worry. If he does, I'll take care of it."

"Well, that wasn't an answer to my question."

No. It wasn't. And I wasn't sure what the answer was. I

didn't know this Marcus. I didn't really know what my leaving did to him, or what his life was like now.

"I hope he stays." It was all I could say.

"Damn, Andrew."

Without turning around, I knew she was shaking her head at me.

"Trust me, I know." I uncrossed my arms, and shook my hands out at my sides as someone else pulled into the parking lot. "I...I was going to try and talk to him as soon as he comes back inside. Assure him that I won't bother him, and keep it...professional."

Vanessa scoffed behind me, and made me grind my teeth while I told myself it wasn't a lie.

"Do you want things to stay professional?" she asked.

"Last time I screwed up and hurt him. If I get to have professional with him, I'll count myself lucky."

Her hand was on my back again, this time with a soft pat before her footsteps sounded behind me as she walked back through the kitchen.

Other staff were arriving now, and I stepped aside as they made their way by me into the kitchen to get ready for the day.

Even though some of them looked at me funny when I only nodded at each of their greetings, I didn't stop looking at Marcus through the rain blurred window of his car.

Somehow, I needed to make this okay.

We shared dreams once. Now I hoped we had one more in common: for him to continue working here.

He didn't leave, even after his windows fogged up, and I couldn't see him as anything other than a vague shape sitting inside.

I didn't leave either.

Every minute gave me both more hope that he would stay, and more fear that he would leave.

But, finally, someone came and asked me a question about one of the machines that was having a problem.

"Come on," I whispered under my breath as I tried to will him to get out of the car and finally make his way back inside.

The last thing I wanted to do was leave my post by the door. I needed to tell him that I would stay out of his way.

More than that, even. I needed to look into his eyes again.

No matter how much it hurt, I needed his eyes the way I needed air. To know that at least they were the same, that they still existed in the man I loved.

Instead of being able to reassure him, instead of being able to see him clearly, I sighed and turned around.

Just like last time, I left Marcus without a word, and headed back inside to fix the machine.

MARCUS

Finally, Shane went back inside.

I got out of my car and stretched in the rain, not caring that the cold and damp would destroy any attempt at decent hair.

The rain smattered along my eyelids. At least the cool splash of it helped to keep the tears at bay.

With another deep breath, I opened my eyes, and made my way back inside.

However, this day would go would determine everything about my future here.

Maybe all the backup on its way to me would help. Maybe it wouldn't be needed. And maybe it would still be far too much for me to look at Shane.

Back when we were together, he liked beer, but I never would have expected him to end up owning a brewery. It wasn't even on my radar of the kind of place where I had any chance of running into him.

Clearly, I didn't know him as well as I thought I did.

For the next hour as we prepared to open the doors, I

managed to avoid Shane. But that thought was lodged in my brain.

How well did I really know the man I thought was the love of my life?

After he left me without a word, and ripped my whole world away with him, it was clear he hid things from me. But, at the time—and for a long time afterward—I believed that he had hidden something that came up suddenly.

The story I told myself about why he left was because something happened that made it necessary for him to go. Something caused him to act the way he had, and, in some way, he just didn't love me enough for me to matter when it happened.

Now, though, I wondered if there was so much more I didn't know. That it wasn't some*thing* I didn't know, it was some*one*: him.

Maybe it wasn't just the end that was steeped in lies. Maybe it was everything about our relationship.

My knees gave out in the same second that the thought ran through me, and I found myself crumpled on the floor with my hands on the seat of a chair, barely keeping my head upright.

"Did you trip? Are you okay?" Layla, one of the other employees, asked as her face came into view.

"Yes, I'm fine. Sorry, just…" I just, what? How could I possibly explain to her what was happening to me?

Swallowing, I shoved myself back up to standing, and, through shallow breaths, I pretended to be someone else.

Based on the way she squinted at me, the smile I gave her was probably brittle and only half-formed. Her mouth opened like she was going to ask about something else, but I turned away from her before she could.

For every minute of preparing, I stayed in constant movement, filling my mind with mundane thoughts about what I was doing.

Oh, those behind-the-bar towels for wiping up felt softer than I expected.

How did a commercial kitchen manage to always look so clean? Maybe one day, far in the future, I would look into having more stainless steel in my home kitchen than I previously planned.

The music was nice, but it was a shame that it drowned out the sound of the rain hitting the skylights.

No matter how inconsequential the thought, I entertained it just to try and stop my traitorous mind from thinking any more about him.

At the same time, I ran songs through my head if I didn't know the one playing over the speakers, and sang along under my breath to the ones I did know.

Finally, through using tricks I wasn't sure would work for even five more minutes than I employed them, I got through it, and the doors were opening.

Right away, Katie and three huge, young men entered, led by Deacon's wide smile, and Katie's smirk under the daggers in her eyes.

He walked so fast across the room to me that I wondered for the first time what he was like on the football field.

I expected him to ask me how I was, or introduce me to his friends. The last thing I expected him to do was what he did.

Deacon wrapped me in a bone-crushing hug, lifting my feet off the floor, and making me squeak.

"Ack." I wanted to tell him to put me down, but I couldn't process being in the air enough to get out the words and his friends were laughing.

"Marcus, my little spoon," Deacon yelled.

"Oh, lord. Deacon, put me down." There. At least I found my voice. That was only because he triggered the highest level of embarrassment I possessed, and therefore the highest level of self-preservation.

"Too much?" he asked, grinning.

With an eye roll, Katie leaned in and gave me a hug, too, before she went back to that threat in her eyes as she studied everyone else in the room, probably trying to figure out who Shane was.

"Nah," one of his buddies said, matching his smile, "that was perfect."

I ran my hands over my face, which felt as hot as the sun, and made me wonder if my deodorant was strong enough.

"Well, I want this dude to know that you have a collection of the hottest boyfriends Seattle has to offer." Deacon stood up straighter, and smiled like he was proud of himself.

"As much as I love that you all are willing to help me with this today," I said, trying not to laugh as I shook my head, "no boyfriends are needed. I don't want to add to the lies in this situation."

Deacon's other friend set his mouth in a grim line like he understood, nodded, and put a hand on my shoulder.

"So, which one is he, and how mean am I allowed to be?" Katie asked, managing to get a smile out of me.

Her eyes brightened, and her smirk turned into something scarier. "Also, Theresa wants me to remind you that she has access to heavy equipment if you decide you need it."

'Be gay, do crimes,' was supposed to be a joke, but Theresa was taking it to be some sort of threatening challenge.

"Okay, if you're all going to stay, would you like the usual tour and tasting?" I asked, taking in a shuddering breath as I tried not to cry, and folding my shaking hands together in front of me.

"Lead the way," they all said, and I started my real day.

But turning around, I made eye contact with Shane where he stood next to the bar, his brows turned up in the middle, and his mouth slightly open.

Part of me wondered if the multiple boyfriends thing would have been a good idea after all.

If Shane looked a little wounded after Deacon's antics, what would he think after a day full of young, beautiful men being just as affectionate?

Holding my head high as we passed him, I chatted with the guys, keeping up a steady banter along with adding all the details I was supposed to about the brewery. I knew I made the right decision.

No matter what happened with this job, whether I would actually be able to handle doing it for very long or not, I didn't want to stoop to Shane's level and become such a liar.

*W*ere all these guys interested in Marcus?

And where did he find them all? 1-800-call-for-a-linebacker?

They were huge.

Well, not all of them. But most of them. And I was pretty sure one of the smaller guys was the running back for the university's football team.

The brewery wasn't new to having people come in that were well-known locally, but this was weird. It was like there was a call out to the whole team for anyone who could come today to do so.

Did they have some strange, day-off drinking ritual we randomly became a part of?

No. They all knew Marcus.

Some of them—especially the touchy-feely, giant, Black guy from the open—were more affectionate than just a casual relationship, too.

Every time one of them touched his hand or grinned up at him, and every time his eyes softened as he smiled at them, or his breath hitched as he spoke to them, my stomach turned.

I didn't have a right for this to hurt.

But it did.

Knowing I was well and truly in his past made my heart ache. Everything in me want to crumple into a ball and cry.

And it wasn't just the guys. Not ten minutes after the open, even more people began to arrive in small groups. And they all knew Marcus, too.

"Did you know he was this popular?" Van asked about halfway through the busiest day we had ever had as Marcus was making the rounds to the tables full of his adoring fans.

I snorted a small laugh.

"Yes and no." There was no clear way to answer that.

Every person who got to know Marcus loved him, and people who had not known him for very long quickly felt comfortable opening up to him in ways they never were with others. He was one of those rare people that everyone just got the impression was trustworthy and good. And they weren't wrong.

But this? This level of special attention for his first day of work at a new place was not what I was expecting, and I couldn't think of anything that rivaled it in the years we were together.

"Thanks, Andrew," Vanessa said to my less-than-helpful response as she shook her head with a good-natured grin, "that clears everything up."

Closer to the end of the day, a familiar voice made me stop in my tracks, and almost drop my end of the keg I was setting in place under the bar.

With a sinking feeling, I slowly stood up, and backed away from the keg so the other people around me could finish what I no longer thought I could.

Sure enough, there she was.

"Hey," Ceecee called out to the large group that had slowly formed in the middle of the room.

Most of them spoke to her, too, and there were hugs all around. Then she looped an arm around Marcus' shoulders, and pulled him in to give him a kiss on the cheek.

Ceecee had her back to me, but I would know her anywhere. She didn't even get dolled up after work to come here. She still had flour on her clothes, and her hair piled on top of her head.

I swallowed.

"Boss?" Layla asked, and I tore my eyes away from my ex and his best friend for a second to look at her before my attention was back to the middle of the room. "Do you want us to finish all this?"

"Yes, please," I said, my throat tight, not bothering to check what she was referring to.

How did I not expect for Ceecee to come in here after I saw Marcus?

When he went out to his car and got on the phone, it had to be to her.

Unless Ceecee had some major personality transplant since I saw her last, of course she and Marcus would still be platonic life mates, the kind of friends who would find a way to support the other when things went sideways.

And this job had clearly gone sideways when he showed up today, and found out I was involved.

No matter how over me he was by now, no one wants to work with their ex.

But he was clearly over me.

One of the large young men leaned toward Marcus at that exact moment, giving him the mooney look only dopey idiots in love got.

I sighed and tried to hold it together even as my stomach flipped again. Adrenaline flooded through me, leaving me shaking, leaning even more heavily against the counter behind me.

Then Ceecee sat down on the other side of the table and looked up.

She made eye contact with me, and I wasn't prepared for the ache it would cause to even look at her.

My heart squeezed tighter in my chest as she stared at me.

Her gaze wasn't as if she was angry with me like I expected.

No. Ceecee looked at me as if every gray, rainy day of her life lived in her eyes at the same time, and they still lacked strength enough to become a storm. The sky in her eyes just wept anemically.

Ceecee tilted her head, and looked away from me.

Dragging in a breath, I mumbled something unintelligible about needing a minute, and wandered back to the kitchen.

Even though I could only partially feel my feet, I made it to a place just out of the way, and leaned against the wall like a washed-up piece of driftwood, lifeless and dulled.

I had to shake this off. I had to be here, with my brain working properly in order to accomplish everything that must be done, and find a way to give Van what she desperately needed.

Marcus being here right now was not helping.

Just his presence in the building was enough to send me into a spin I was beginning to fear would end with me crumpled on the floor and useless to everyone.

But this? The full-on assault with the deadly weapon of his friends was enough to make that broken mess version of me come faster and shatter me even worse.

Why?

I didn't know why having them all show up and clearly demonstrate to me how many people in his life loved him was worse than making eye contact and seeing every dream I ever had for the future in his eyes.

Groaning—or more like whimpering—I ran my hands over my face and ground the heels of my palms into my eyes.

"H-hey," Marcus said, his voice stuttering over the word as

my eyes popped open, and my hands dropped to my sides leaving me staring at him.

MARCUS

Oh, God, what was I supposed to say now? Why did I even open my fat mouth?

Shane could have gone on forever and not known I was here watching him fall apart. But no, I had to go and say something, and force both of us into this messed up moment blank stares.

I was still a fool.

"Um…Sorry. Just…uh, Vanessa wants to talk to you." Crap. None of that made sense.

Good job, self, you suck.

Even my inner voice was beating up on me tonight.

"Yeah," he said, his voice as thin as his eyes. The red from rubbing at them swam with the wet that I assumed was a response to the same rough treatment of his own face. "I'll…go find her."

Nodding, wondering what I should do with my hands as they hung limp at my sides, I stepped back, and moved to the other side of the kitchen to get more limes out of the refrigerator. Which was the reason I came back here.

I should've just stayed out on the floor, and left someone else to come back here. I should've paid attention to where Shane went.

But stupid me, I spent most the night trying to avoid knowing where he was, and trying only to focus on the person directly in front of me. Not just because we were so busy and so many of my friends and their friends showed up, but because it was safer that way. And I was more likely to survive the night.

The bustling of so many employees doing their jobs drowned out any clue I had as to whether Shane was back out on the floor. And once again, my traitor self decided to turn back and look for him.

Why I thought it would help me to know where he was now that it was too late to help me avoid him, I didn't know. But it shot me in butt, too.

He was still leaning against the counter, staring at me, his eyes red, his chest rising and falling in staccato bursts of movement.

Snapping my head back around, I almost lost my footing, but managed to right myself as I made my way to do what I needed to.

Please be gone, I begged of him in my head.

After standing there like a broken mannequin without the ability to move my hands and turning back to look at him, I didn't want to navigate around him again. That didn't even include the epic mumbling nonsense that spilled out of my mouth in his presence. Repeating the disaster of talking to him in the kitchen was the last thing I wanted to do tonight.

Who was I kidding? The last thing I *ever* wanted to do was navigate around him at all.

I still didn't know how I was supposed to handle doing this long term.

My friends couldn't organize a massive influx of themselves to act as buffers every time I worked. They couldn't even do a steady trickle. People had lives.

Even now, I was well aware that if this was football season, Deacon and all his teammates wouldn't have been able to spend all day loitering around a brewery's tasting room without getting in trouble.

The only reason it was really working was the shuffling in and out of different people like they were on shifts. That and they were all being very careful about their drinking.

We were serving a lot of food.

But the night was almost over. I only had a couple more hours here, and then…

Stumbling out of the refrigerator, I was relieved not to see Shane still there. But that was short lived as the logistical reality of closing time dawned on me.

Unless Shane left without helping to close, there was a lot less likelihood of me being able to avoid him completely once my friends weren't here for interference.

Part of the joys of this job were the few long days I had to work per week which gave me most of the mid-week off, like a nurse's schedule. That *had* been a good thing when I agreed to work here.

Now, though, knowing that we all worked open to close these days the tasting room was open made my heart constrict in my chest all over again.

Even Ceecee wouldn't be able to shield me after the doors were closed to the public, and we all started getting ready to go home ourselves.

I wandered out of the back and to the bar, delivering the limes to one of the waiting bartenders.

"Thanks, Marcus," he said with a smile, but all I could do was nod in response.

My head was filled with dread, and I scanned the crowd until I found Ceecee sitting with all her friends.

Before I got back over to them, her eyes met mine, her brow

furrowed, and she was half out of her chair by the time I got to her.

"What happened?" she asked, and the others around the table fell silent.

"I didn't think about closing," I said, the most pressing of the issues that sent all my common sense screaming in panic as it fled my brain.

"You'll be okay," she said, standing all the way up, and wrapping her arms around me. "I'll be waiting in your car."

"Ceecee," I said, hugging her back. I didn't want her to do that.

"Don't argue," she said, pulling back and fixing me with a stern look. "Tee already knows I'll be home late, by the way."

She held her hand out to me, palm up, with a half-smile that made me roll my eyes and love her more.

The others laughed as I fished my keys out of my pocket and put them in her hand.

"Okay, now that that's handled," Katie said, a wicked grin on her face, "someone still needs to point out this very bad man to me."

I blinked and looked at Ceecee who avoided my gaze.

"No one's told you who he is?" I asked, not understanding the odd way everyone else was acting. Even Deacon's teammates were looking down at the table with wide eyes.

She looked to Ceecee and the others with a raised brow and pursed lips.

"Everyone seems to think that if I know, I'll do something crazy." She widened her eyes and wiggled her fingers like jazz hands, which actually managed to get a chuckle out of me.

"He's…" I looked up and quickly checked the room, "not in here at the moment. But Ceecee can point him out to you."

Ceecee tried to tell me to rethink that with her eyes, but I didn't care if she pointed him out to Katie or anyone else.

"Listen," I said, shaking my head at Ceecee and gesturing for her to sit back down, "all of you have done this all day. I doubt he's so oblivious that he hasn't noticed. He must know something's up. As long as no one hurts him, I don't care."

"I kind of want to see what he looks like, too," one of Deacon's teammates said, looking around as if he could figure it out without anyone saying anything.

"Dude," one of the other guys said.

"We're supposed to be intimidating someone. It would be nice to know if he's built like the Rock."

That had everyone laughing.

"No," I said, trying to imagine Shane that huge, and just coming up with big old nopes in my head. "He's not that big. He's...perfect."

My last word was barely a whisper, but they all heard it judging by the sad looks on their faces, and the pat Ceecee gave my hand.

"Still?" Campbell asked, his voice soft and full of understanding.

I sighed and looked up, seeing Shane come from one of the offices talking with Vanessa. His shirtsleeves were rolled up, showing off his forearms. The lighting made him look as delicious as all the food, and as intoxicating as all the alcohol.

"Yeah. Unfortunately." I nodded toward Shane, not taking my eyes off him, and the others all turned to look.

"Hot damn, Marcus. That's him?" Katie asked, her voice appreciative.

"Blue shirt," Ceecee said, her voice dripping venom while Katie nodded. "Yeah. That's him."

"We could take him," Deacon's friend said, which started a whole conversation amongst them about who on the team would or would not be able to beat Shane up if they so wanted to.

I was no longer listening. I was caught in the way the blue of his shirt looked against his skin, turning my real-life ex into some kind of soft-focus photo I wouldn't be able to forget even after I never saw him again.

Because that's how this would end. Whether I kept working here, or not. One day I would no longer see Shane. One day he'd be just as much a faraway memory as he was yesterday. This time, though, I would have the added burden of knowing that the only reason he was a memory and not a part of my life anymore was because he just up and left.

In all the years in between, I thought there was a reason. But if there had been, he'd have said something by now.

So that left the only thing that made any sense.

When Shane left me and told everyone we knew to lie about the circumstances of his leaving, it was because he was sick of me. That was the cleanest break as far as he was concerned. It was because I wasn't worth the time for him to explain.

SHANE

"**V**an, please," I said, trying to keep my voice even. No one else should know about our ongoing struggle over this. If any of them knew, they might doubt us, the business, all manner of things, and we might end up with a mass exodus of employees. "I know you need this, and you know I want to give you this. I am trying. Just give me some more time."

"Andrew," she said, heaving a sigh and coming to a sudden stop. "I know you will find a way. And I want you to. More than anything. But I don't know how much longer I can keep this going. It's…"

Her eyes started to swim with unshed tears, and she took a few deep breaths as I put a hand on her shoulder.

"Too much. It's all too much. I know, Van. I'm sorry. I'll make this work, and you won't have to do all this anymore. As it is, you won't have to leave California to come back here again. I promise."

"I know you'll make it work, Andrew. That's why I keep waiting. Thanks." She gave me a watery smile, and looked past my shoulder. The look in her eyes changed from the sharp edge of grief to a soft speculation. "Or should I call you Shane?"

"Don't start," I said, shaking my head and walking past her as she managed a small laugh.

"Why did you change it when you came to California?" she asked, sounding genuinely curious.

"Mom refused to call me anything other than the first name she gave me. The only people who knew me as Shane were here or already gone, so...I just thought it would be easier not to have to hear it every day."

Now it was her turn to pat my shoulder.

"Did your dad call you that, too?" she asked, her voice as small as the little tasting cups we used.

"Yeah, but it wasn't so much Dad that..." I couldn't finish the sentence.

Because it wasn't at all the memory of my father—gone a year by the time I left the state—that made me want to use my given first name again. To be honest, it wasn't my mother, either. And Vanessa knew it.

"Van," I said, my voice hard.

"What?" she asked, lifting her hands in a shrug, the picture of innocence.

"Please don't try to make something happen. Look at him." I gestured over my shoulder with my head, refusing to turn around, yet knowing exactly where Marcus was in the room. "He has a life—a very full one—that doesn't include me."

"I just don't understand why you didn't tell me before how the breakup happened." She shook her head, watching him over my shoulder.

"Because you would have tried to change it, just like I can see your brain trying to come up with a way to make it different now."

"Andrew," she said, looking back at me, "you don't know what I would have done, or what I'm thinking. But we both know that you need to talk to him. Tell him the truth. It isn't the same now."

"No, it isn't. But I'm pretty sure I don't want to run afoul of any of the giant guys that have been flirting with him all day."

She rolled her eyes, and shook her head.

"I'm choosing to ignore your terrible, accidental pun, and I'm only going to point out that every single one of those football players who you think have been flirting with him today is straight." She raised her brows as I recoiled, and walked away, leaving me dumbfounded.

They couldn't be straight. If they were that would mean that…

With a quick twist, I looked back toward Marcus Mason, the love of my life, and found all the eyes at the table full of his friends focused on me while he walked over to the bar.

Ceecee's eyes narrowed, but it wasn't in fury this time. It was in calculation.

All the guys around the table looked at me as if they were sizing me up for a challenge on a field, not as a potential rival for someone they were into. Except one who was definitely not a football player. Although tall, he was too thin. That guy was looking at me as if he were sad for me. It was the face of someone at a funeral, and it made me swallow down a lump because I was too familiar with that look.

The other woman who was with the group was looking at me, too. But she launched herself from her seat, deftly avoiding the grasping hands of the others as she made a beeline to me, a smirk on her face.

I froze.

My brain abandoned me as I stared at the approaching woman, my hands wanting to shake. I folded them together in front of me, and just waited for whatever was about to befall me. For some reason, I felt like I was a rabbit being hunted by an eagle. Her gaze was so direct, her face so quirked into the look of someone with private information. And there wasn't a single thing I could think of to avoid this.

"Katie," Ceecee said, having caught up with her friend a mere five feet in front of me, and grabbing her by the arm. With a quick swivel, she turned Katie away from me, but Ceecee kept her eyes on me. "You can't right now. Marcus asked us not to."

"Come on, Ceecee," Katie said, twisting around to look back at me. "I just want to know for sure."

"And I'm telling you," Ceecee said, her focus solely on Katie as she started to lead her back toward the table, "everything there was to know happened a long time ago. If there's anything else, it isn't up to us."

Even after they were out of earshot, their words drowned out by the general noise of the room, I didn't move. Instead, I stared at Ceecee's back, and wondered what she meant. What had Katie intended to find out?

My eyes strayed back to Marcus, again, taking in the way his cheeks lost their color, and the way he leaned across the table to point at Katie gave me some ideas about what was going on.

Katie was told something today, something about Marcus and me, and she wanted to interrogate me.

Fine. I wanted to know some things, too.

Right now, Ceecee was running interference. Marcus was standing there, too, but maybe I would get another chance to see Katie. Maybe then we could have the conversation she wanted to have.

And maybe I could find a way to make this connection to Marcus' life make up for the last one.

Taking a much clearer breath than I had since I saw him for the first time that morning, I turned around and got back to work.

Maybe if I could find a way not to hurt him again—maybe even do something good for him—I could clear up whatever curse was following me, and stopping me from doing what needed to be done for Vanessa.

Van was counting on me. Our whole family was. Her

husband and kids. She was my last surviving relative. And I knew I was running out of time. Somehow, I had to find a way before she couldn't wait anymore.

It was probably wishful thinking, begging the universe to give me any chance at all that explained the odd feeling in my stomach that I needed to make things right with Marcus before I figured this out for Van. But I couldn't shake the idea.

"Okay, then," I said out loud to no one, and got back to work while ideas raced through my head.

"I promise, Ceecee," I whispered into her shoulder as she hugged me one last time before walking out the door.

"Okay." She stepped back from me, and held up her phone and my keys, raising her brows as if I didn't *just* assure her that I knew I could call her if I needed her for any reason because she'd be out in my car waiting for me.

She finally turned and walked out while I watched her.

This needed to happen. There was no way around it. I was a big boy, and could handle my ex being in the same building as me all on my own.

Yeah. Sure, I could.

All I needed to do was turn around, and get to work.

Not much to it.

Something I had done a thousand times before in other jobs.

This wasn't different.

Why would this be different?

It wasn't a big deal. It was just working with zero buffer from the only man I had ever loved…

I was screwed.

Swallowing, I balled my hands into fists, focused on the floor at my feet, and turned around to get to work.

All I had to do was not look up.

That sounded like a solid plan.

Until I swiveled with my hands full of dishes to take to the kitchen, and almost ran right into someone.

"Oh, I'm so sorry," I said, stumbling backward, trying to regain my balance even as their hand shot out to grab my forearm and steady me.

I didn't need to look up now. Even if it hadn't been for the way his touch froze my arm, as if he were made of ice, I knew that hand. I knew the way the fingers fit around my arm, the darker brown freckle on his dark skin near the base of his thumb, even the blue shirt I tried not to stare at all night long.

Finally, after a moment of neither of us moving, or even breathing, I raised my eyes and looked into Shane's.

He gulped down a heavy breath.

"Marcus."

And that was all he said. He just said my name, and it was enough to make me think about calling Ceecee.

The way he said it, it was as if no time had passed, and we were back in my room the night before he left for good, saying my name right after, "I love you," like he always did.

When we were still teenagers, after dating for six months and twelve days, he said he loved me for the first time.

I didn't say it back. My tongue was lodged in my throat, choking me with all the things I wanted to say to him in response. There were just too many.

And because of the delay, his face fell, and he said my name in a pleading tone, asking me for something, anything. What he got then were tears and rambling words that somewhere in there included me returning the sentiment.

Every single time after that, when we traded I-love-you's, he always followed it up with saying my name in a voice that said so much more.

Now, years after the good night that I didn't realize meant goodbye, he did it again. He said my name in a way that meant so much more.

Pulling my arm out of his grasp, I managed not to drop the load of dishes in my hands.

"Don't," I said, managing to eke out one of the many words stopping my tongue this time, and stomped away.

After working like the lives of everyone I cared about were on the line, we were almost done, and I was wiping down my last table.

But that damn blue shirt appeared out of the corner of my eye.

"I think we should talk," he said, avoiding my name entirely.

"Why?" I asked, not looking at him, just doubling my efforts at wiping up.

"Please, Marcus," he said, his voice low and sounding like he was exhausted, which only managed to make me angry.

"No." I turned and stared into the face I loved more than any other in the world.

Even though that was still true, and would probably stay true, I finally borrowed enough of Ceecee's fury to say what I needed to. "After you left me without a word, with nothing but secondhand lies from everyone we knew, you don't get to tell me we have anything left to talk about."

"But—what?" he asked, shaking his head, and managing to act as if that wasn't what happened.

"There is nothing left to talk about, Andrew," I said, using the name I had never in my life called him. If he erased me so easily, I would return the favor. "Unless you have something you need to tell me about my work tonight?"

He paused, opened his mouth to say something, and closed it again. Finally, he took a deep breath and a step back.

"Um, no. You did a good job." His eyes were looking at something just above my head, and his body was rigid.

I nodded to my new boss, and tried to remember that's all he really was now as I walked away, not caring if the table wasn't done. Because I was more than done.

Making my way to the back, I tossed the towel into the laundry bin, grabbed my things, and stalked out into the night.

On my way out, someone might have tried to speak with me. They might not have. All I could hear was my own blood pounding through my head and into my ears.

Ceecee was in my car, her eyes shining in the light of her phone as she did whatever she was doing on it to pass the time.

No one else had left the building yet. I was alone as I made my way to my car, and tried to fill my body with the cool air of the night all around me.

Part of me knew it wouldn't lessen the heat racing through my veins that screamed in equal parts anger and love, and all of it had his name ripping through me.

I swung open my car door, and collapsed onto the seat.

Ceecee put her phone down, and blinked at me in the bright of the dome light.

"You want me to drive?" she asked, grabbing my hand.

Twisting my hand around to thread my fingers with hers, I held on like she was the only thing keeping me from floating away on the sea of feelings boiling inside me.

"No, I need to drive." I swung my legs in the rest of the way, and shut the door, plunging us back into darkness. "But maybe keep talking to me about other stuff. And I don't think I'll turn on the radio. I'll either cry, or drive way too fast."

She laughed, but it was forced. I pretended not to notice as I started the car.

Because she was the best, Ceecee did as I asked, then told me I had no choice but to stay the night at her house.

"As long as Theresa doesn't tempt me too much with that

heavy equipment," I said, and she finally laughed for real. Although this time it had a sharp edge.

I hoped she kept that edge, because I was going to need to borrow it.

"Tomorrow," I said, in the middle of her sentence about Theresa's latest project away from remodeling their building, "I'm going back to work, and I'm keeping this job until I find another one."

"Good," she said, her voice chipper. "You can always come work for me."

"We both know that you can no longer afford me." I smiled at her, and she patted my hand.

Neither of us mentioned that my statement was only true because the brewery gave me such a big raise and a fancy title. This job included more work I was supposed to be doing than just what I did tonight, and because I was stupid and optimistic, I went and spent all my savings.

Maybe I wouldn't have time to get to the marketing portion of the job they hired me to do, but having it on my resume should help me get another like it.

"Do you think I should list Vanessa or him as my contact person?" I asked, interrupting her again, choking on his name, and opting for just him instead.

"I would use him. If he says anything negative, it would be a great excuse to punch him in the face."

Now I laughed with her.

Yep. I was going back. And I was taking that edge with me.

At this rate, I wouldn't survive.

After not sleeping at all, I dragged myself into work the next morning. All night, I thought about Marcus, and there was no one I could turn to about him. I spent three hours poring over every financial document I could think of, even some I knew wouldn't be helpful.

I tried to come up with something. Anything. But I was out of ideas, and I was quickly running out of time.

Now, the one damn thing I had some vague hope in— making things right with Marcus— was all but destroyed. For some reason, I thought that would matter to my inability to think my way out of the problem with Vanessa.

Finally, I pushed back from my desk, and rubbed my hands roughly over my face.

My sleepless brain was mush, and looking at all these figures wasn't doing a thing for me.

So, I heaved myself up from the desk, and wandered into the experimental room, taking in the many smells that wafted through as different ingredients were pulled out to use in small batches.

Our brewmaster was making notes in one of the logs as I made my way over to her.

"Hey, Zeda," I said, leaning against one of the stools along the work counter. "Any wins? Losses?"

"You always ask for the wins first, but then don't give me time to answer you."

I was too tired to puzzle out what she thought that said about me.

"And? What does that mean?" But I still wanted to know what she thought.

"Most likely that you're always hoping for the best, but don't believe you actually deserve it." She finished writing her notes, and looked up at me while her words stabbed me right in the heart.

"Ouch," I said, holding a hand to my chest to cover the wound she delivered.

"Truth can hurt, but that isn't even the meanest thing I've said to you this week. What's up, Boss? You look like crap."

I couldn't help laughing as I lifted the hand on my heart to my face, and rubbed my eyes.

"Like always, thank you, Zeda."

She just cocked her head to the side with a smile that may as well have been a shrug.

"We're both going to ignore your diagnosis of what ails me," I said, to which her mouth turned into a thin line, "and instead we're going to come up with some brilliant new beer that will double our income. So you can save my butt. Because right now, I need a win, Zeda. A big one."

The whole time I was talking, her eyes narrowed further and further. That thin line of her mouth turned down at the corners more and more.

Maybe I said too much.

"You going to explain that to me, Boss? We got a problem?"

Well, crap. I screwed that all up. No one knew what was going on, and I needed to keep it that way.

"Please pretend I didn't say anything. It isn't a problem for anyone other than me. It's fine. I just need a win right now. For personal reasons. I really wanted to have something to give to Van at her party in three weeks."

She shook her head, looking up at the wall of tanks and all the various experiments we were conducting.

"Even for me, three weeks is pushing it. How am I supposed to have genius strike at just the right time? And it wouldn't be ready to taste by then."

"Z, I'm sorry. I am. I don't want to push more work on you or pile on pressure. But if you have some magic idea in that notebook, it would be great to pull it out. Because I am too messed up in my brain right now to think about even matching my clothes." I couldn't tell her why I needed an idea right now. But this truth I could tell her no problem. According to her, I already looked like it.

"All that in your brain, is that why you look so bad?"

I squeezed my eyes shut and sighed.

"Can you give me specific things you think I can do to make me look a little less crappy?

She laughed and turned away from me, shaking her head. All that just drove in another stab.

"Thanks, Zeda. Keep me updated on any new ideas, or things that work out. If I can manage to think of anything, I'll let you know."

With a wave of her hand over her head, her back still to me, she went to the bins and pulled out a vial of vanilla extract.

I knew her well enough to recognize it as her cue that I needed to leave her alone, so I headed back to my office.

Zeda was a lot of things. Odd. Blunt. Not exactly someone people loved having at parties. Honest to the point of murder.

One of the best noses of anyone I had ever met, and that included sommeliers. And absolutely brilliant at making beer.

She was also one of the best friends I had ever had. She followed me back here from California after she was integral to us starting Mason Jar Brewery down there. But she didn't want to be a partner.

More than all of that, though, she was one of the reasons I stayed even remotely okay through the mess I was when I first had to move down there.

Not telling my friends much so they wouldn't try and stop me from going, left me alienated from most of them. Zeda picked up the pieces.

But now there was all this I couldn't tell her.

If she found out that the "Mason guy" she heard all about was Marcus, and he was working here after we named the place after him…she would force me to turn the world upside down to get him back. And that wasn't what Marcus wanted.

He made that clear.

Nothing was clear to me anymore except that.

All our most popular beers were wild ideas I had that Zeda made work, and sometimes made better.

Blackberry. Huckleberry. Nothing that made any sense when I was yammering about them to her.

I wasn't lying, though, when I told her my brain was broken. I couldn't sleep. I couldn't focus. There was zero chance I could be creative.

Maybe I could find a way to get other people who worked here, other brains like Zeda's working on ideas for me.

Opening the door to my office, I froze.

Looking up at the mirrored window on my door, I saw the reflection of the room behind me.

This door, a beautiful piece of history from the days of prohibition, was from an old speakeasy. Vanessa's friend—who was the manager of the brewery down in California—found it for us at some antique shop in Texas or somewhere. Someone could see out, but no one could see in.

Now, though, it was my office door. And the reflection it showed me was of mine and my cousin's legally-founded brewery where my ex-boyfriend stood by a table, staring at my back.

He made eye contact with me through the mirror, and I saw nothing on his face.

Yesterday, every time I looked at him there were so many emotions flitting across his face it was hard to track them all, let alone puzzle out what they all meant.

Yesterday, his eyes were overwhelming. Now they were not just underwhelming, but shocking in their lack of feeling.

Did he feel nothing for me now?

Was that where we were at?

If he felt indifferent to me now, it really was over. More completely over and done than I ever thought we would be.

Swallowing down a sob, I went into my office and shut the door.

Looking through the glass, I placed a hand on it, rubbing my thumb along the image of his hair. It wasn't what I wanted. I wanted to touch him, hold him, beg him to forgive me. I wanted to tell him it could all be different now.

The only thing I was waiting for to make the move back here permanent was over now.

I wanted to tell him that I named the brewery for him.

So much. I wanted to tell him so much.

But instead, I cried silent tears alone in my office while I stole a chance to look at him, and remember when he loved me.

MARCUS

Could I manage to do this every single day until I got another job?

Shane had yet to make another appearance out of his office, but I knew he was in there. And that was like a guillotine made especially for my heart following me around as I worked.

Tonight, I still had a trickle of people checking on me, and every time I stepped away for a breather, there was another text to answer from Ceecee.

But it wasn't the same influx as yesterday.

For that I was grateful.

Having them there as a buffer was a huge benefit, but I couldn't do that every day. And I needed to know if I could handle it long enough to do what I needed to.

Plus, the day I was supposed to be working on the other aspects of my job and not be out here in the tasting room would make it impossible for anyone to help me.

I couldn't just jump into that without having any moments on my own.

All of the sudden, in my twenties, I was returned to a little kid who had to walk to the park with friends before I was allowed to walk alone.

"Marcus," Vanessa said, pulling me out of my own head.

"Yeah? Is there something you need me to do?" I asked, it was a good time for her to pull me away. Everyone in the tasting room was taken care of, there weren't tours scheduled for the next half hour, and the staff was keeping up well with the current number of people.

"Tomorrow you'll be doing your other work," she said, smiling as she put away the reservation book she was just writing in, "and I wanted to bring you back to talk to Zeda so that you're ready for it. Should we do that later, or…?"

"Sure. It's a great time right now." I smiled back and started toward the experimental room.

From the first time I met Zeda, the idea of working with her made me think there were only two options for how it would pan out: fantastic, or terrible. There would be no in-between. Zeda didn't seem like an in between person.

I liked her so far. But I wasn't entirely sure when she was joking.

"Well?" Vanessa said as we walked, one brow raised in question.

How honest could I be with her?

Trying to pull time out of the suddenly-thin air, I smiled. But her face didn't change, and it was clear she wasn't going to let me out of this one.

"Fine," I said, crossing my fingers in my mind that she would let it go.

"Just fine?" She laughed, but there was a little tinge of hurt in it.

"So much has kept me moving, I haven't really had time to think about it all. Ask me after a few days off."

Her laugh that time was real, and lacked the touch of pain it had before.

"That's fair. But I *am* going to ask you again."

"Also fair." Maybe by the time she asked me again I would have another job lined up, and I could tell her the truth.

Neither of the owners really wanted me working here.

There was zero chance Shane really wanted me here, and, once Vanessa knew about my real history with Shane, she wouldn't either.

Besides, no matter how excited I was about this job at the start, I no longer wanted to stay either.

It hurt too much.

I opened the door for both of us to walk through into the experimental room. It was as shiny and metallic like the kitchen, even if it had an odd, mad scientist vibe to it that the kitchen didn't.

My nose was assaulted to the point I had to squeeze the bridge of my nose and shut my eyes to keep from sneezing the moment we walked in the door.

"Zeda," Vanessa said next to me, shaking her head, "what is that?"

"Oh, hi, Vanessa. Hi, Marcus. Sorry. I had a little spill of pepper." Zeda appeared from behind one of the machines and shrugged.

"Pepper is in beer? And pepper can do this?" I asked, my eyes still wanting to water. It was as if the pepper had infused itself with every single molecule in the air, and was beating the crap out of my olfactory sensors.

"Well, it was a pepper extract, so a little spill is kind of like a giant spill of the kind of pepper you're used to." She didn't look apologetic, and, for a second, I had trouble understanding how someone who wasn't bothered by this situation was in charge of new flavors.

"Before you ask, Marcus," Zeda looked at me, a smirk forming on her face, "some people are more susceptible to pepper than others, and I'm guessing now that I am not one and you are."

"Good bet," I said, giving up all my attempts to pretend this wasn't torture, and holding my nose closed like a five-year-old about to jump in a lake.

Zeda laughed and Vanessa, who seemed to be over it now, just cringed at me in sympathy.

"Maybe it would be best to have this discussion tomorrow," Vanessa said.

"I'm in here now. May as well make it matter." This was awful, but I really hoped that tomorrow I wouldn't have to spend as much time in here if we got it done. That way, I could avoid any lingering overdose of pepper.

"You sure?" Vanessa asked at the same time Zeda said, "Fine by me."

"So, what you're going to need to do with me is get the list of seasonal flavors we're playing with, and come up with some ideas for them, to get them distributed, hopefully. The other thing is, we need to go over the flavor profiles of every beer we have so you know what is in each one, and can do some marketing with those as well."

"None of that sounds like a problem, although I'm curious why you think all the marketing needs to change if it's working so far." I was more than curious. The whole reason they hired me was to come up with some big new ideas for marketing when they were already doing well enough to warrant opening this brewery on top of the one they had in California.

"Do you want me to tell you," Zeda said, deadpan, "or would you rather have a meeting with Vanessa in the office to go over it?"

I tried to look apologetic at Zeda, even though she said it like it didn't matter one way or the other, because the sooner I could get out of this room, the better.

"Office?" I asked, my voice nasally as I increased the pressure of holding my nose.

The idea of escaping this smell, instead of offering the relief of a light at the end of the tunnel, made it harder to try and ignore how much it bothered me.

"Come on," Vanessa said, laughing and patting me on the back.

"See you tomorrow," Zeda said, waving and turning back to whatever she was doing before we got here.

As soon as we stepped outside and the door closed behind us, I took a deep breath in and coughed as the remainders of the pepper smell that were stuck in my nose hit me with another blast.

"Do you think you're allergic?" Vanessa asked. "Are you sure you can do this?"

"I'm not allergic. No other spices don't do this to me. Just black pepper. Why would she try black pepper in beer?" I shook my head, and tried more deep breaths, keeping my eyes shut so they didn't water.

"Most of us learned quick to stay out of her way. You would be surprised what little touches of things she puts into some of the beer to make some other flavor stand out more, or to tame something. I don't even try and understand it all anymore."

Nodding, although I didn't really get it, I finally tried to open my eyes, hoping they wouldn't water.

But when I opened my eyes, I was faced with Shane as he walked right for us, his head down and his eyes on the floor.

I stood up straighter and fumbled at my eyes, hoping to wipe away any hint that I was so bothered just a second ago.

"Andrew," Vanessa said, and he snapped his eyes up to her, his gaze landing on me and staying there as he stopped walking. "Good. We need to talk to Marcus."

We?

Oh, crap. This wasn't what I thought I was voting for when I opted for an office meeting away from that terrible room. Now, one of the options would be torture to my senses, and the other would be torture to my heart.

I needed to get out of the building. A meeting with Shane might end with me yelling at him.

But he just nodded, his eyes still on me, exhaustion and pain hanging off him like he made his clothes out of them.

No matter what he looked like, I kept my face impassive, refusing to have anything spark sympathy in me on his behalf.

"Did you just come from seeing Zeda?" he asked, his voice a croak that I recognized from stressed and sleepless Shane, which wasn't something that happened often when we knew each other. Except for when his dad passed away.

What happened to him?

No. I didn't care. Of course not…

I mentally slapped myself, telling my stupid heart to stop caring.

"Yeah," Vanessa said, even though he was still looking at me, "but we can't go back in there right now. She had a black pepper spill."

"Oh, no. Marcus," he said, stepping forward before I realized what he was doing, and putting a hand on my arm. The heat of his touch through my sleeve was just as searing as if I touched it to a hot stove. I flinched.

He snatched his hand back, folding it in with the other one in front of him in a white-knuckle grip.

"Are you okay?" he asked, and it sounded like there were a thousand words hidden in that question.

I swallowed, and it took me a protracted moment to answer. That left Vanessa enough time to look back and forth between us, her brows raised.

"Fine," I said, not knowing what, exactly, I was answering anymore.

SHANE

My hand still didn't feel right. I was more aware of the ridges in my palm than ever before because that was where I touched him.

Of course, I knew enough to know that I was just being a fool for him. Again.

Even after all this time and everything that went on between us and in my life, just touching my hand to his arm reduced me to feeling like an inadequate teenager who didn't know how to handle falling in love.

"Wow," Vanessa said, her eyes rested on me, looking like she was about to spring a trap, "you know each other really well."

"Knew," Marcus said, his voice hard, "we knew each other pretty well. But how well can you really ever know someone? I have learned that some people will always have secrets, even if you don't expect them to. And some will, even when they promise they won't."

Vanessa's eyes were wide, and her mouth hung open. Marcus kept his cold gaze on mine the entire time he spoke. I wasn't sure if he was aware of Van's reaction.

Trying for a chuckle, it sounded like a hollow grunt before I said, "Well, we should go have that discussion."

I turned around and walked toward my office, trying to find a way to talk to him about professional things like I *needed* to when all I *wanted* to do was sit him down and force him to listen to me begging.

Not that it would help. Not that he didn't have every right to hate me. But every comment, every hard look, made it even more difficult to pretend that I didn't want to apologize. It also made it more difficult to pretend that he didn't skewer me with every arrow he shot at me.

When I got to my office, I pulled open the door and waited for both of them to file inside.

The only problem with that was that my office wasn't big. To get past him to my seat, I scooted close enough to Marcus that a twitch of my fingers would have been enough to run my hands through his hair.

And I wanted to feel his hair running through my fingers so badly that I curled them into fists to stop myself.

Maybe getting slapped with a sexual harassment lawsuit wasn't a great way to keep him from quitting.

Once I was settled in my chair on the other side of the desk, I gestured to Van to get started because I needed a few minutes to prepare to speak.

"You asked why we want to do a marketing realignment," Van said, getting right to the point, which managed to drag me back to professional just a little bit. "Well, our California location is doing very well, and this one has done alright with the same campaigns. But not as well."

She turned her gaze to me, letting me take it from there, because much of what was going on was up to me to tell him.

I looked to Marcus who slowly let his eyes meet mine.

Whatever else I planned on saying ran far away from me under his watch. There couldn't be anymore lies between us.

That was the only way I could have any chance to keep him working here, and keep him in my life even in this small way.

"Vanessa's husband is sick, and she needs to be home with him and their kids," I said. Van's eyes widened even as her mouth pinched, and I knew she was fighting tears.

Marcus shot Van a concerned look, and touched the back of her hand where it rested on the arm of her chair. She just blinked in response.

"The California brewery has a new manager and some distribution deals. But this location doesn't have any distribution yet, and we need to find a way for them both to make enough that I can buy Van out so she can stay home. Traveling back and forth from California is a problem for her, and right now we can't afford to hire a manager here in Washington so I can easily do the coverage for both."

He nodded, and I could almost see all the information I dumped on him getting processed through his mind as he tried to come up with something to help the situation.

"You don't plan on splitting your time between here and California, then?" Marcus asked, his voice sounding as if his throat was tight.

I swallowed even as I tried not to get my hopes up that his comment meant what I thought it might.

"No. I've moved back up here completely. This last trip was to tie up what I needed to finish down there. I would like to limit my trips to once a quarter, and for not as long. But right now, I can't do that."

"When do you need to figure something out by?" he asked.

"Tomorrow?" Van said, her voice low.

"Right," he said, his brow furrowed as he stared down at his hands.

"And I know this is a lot to take in," I said, sweating again, and wishing I could just not talk anymore, "and not what you were expecting. But this is the truth. We need your help."

He snapped his eyes up to look at me, taking in a shuddering breath.

"But we have been trying to come up with a plan for months as things have grown worse," Vanessa said, looking away from both of us as she swiped at her cheeks, "and I...neither of us have come up with something that's worked out. And I can't be here if something happens."

Marcus nodded and my heart ached.

Vanessa knew from my own experience what it was to get the sudden phone call and struggle to get away. In her case it was so much worse because she had kids.

"Zeda said something about new beers. Is that part of your plan, too?" he asked, and, for a second, I realized how close we were to throwing a hail Mary pass, and hoping for the best.

The universe had a sick sense of humor to put Marcus in the place of the person who was essentially a prayer on my part.

"Yes and no," I said, trying to keep in the bitter laugh that wanted to come out of my mouth. "She thinks it would help, but I haven't been able to get anything to work on that front."

"Andrew and Zeda came up with all of what we currently have," Van said, and my knee-jerk reaction was to argue. Van was the reason we formed the business. She set up all of it, and developed everything we had that brought in money. "I am zero help when it comes to anything creative."

But I couldn't argue with her there. We came up with things, she saw them implemented, and got them out to people.

Now, the only reason I could even imagine her leaving was because she set up all the systems we operated by.

Although systems weren't going to get her paid out so she could take care of her family.

"So, your creativity well has run so dry that Zeda is in there messing around with pepper?" Marcus asked, his nose scrunching up at even the word.

I couldn't stop the small laugh that popped out of me that time, although it was less twisted with bitterness thankfully.

His head popped up, and the way he looked at me for a second reminded me of a long time ago. Then a cold wall slammed over his features again, and he looked off into the corner.

"Marcus," Van said, his name snapping me back to the reality we found ourselves in, to the precarious position Van and I were in, and that we were handing it all to him. All I could do was hope he wouldn't deliberately shatter it because I screwed up, "we don't expect you to be able to fix everything. We're just hoping you can help."

With a nod of his head, she relaxed, but I wasn't so sure it didn't mean he would run screaming from the building, and laugh as it all fell down around me.

"Just one question," he asked, which Van sat up to listen to even as dread pooled in my stomach for some reason I couldn't fully identify, "why don't you take on another partner?"

And there it was. The big problem.

"Someone has offered," I said, trying not to let their face flash into my mind, "but to say it isn't ideal would be an understatement."

His brow furrowed, a tiny line appearing in the middle as Van pursed her lips and let out a huff.

"This person has made their intentions known," Van said.

"Well, that's one way to put it," I muttered, dragging a hand over my face.

"I get the feeling no one wants to do business with them?" Marcus asked, a careful tone to his voice as he looked back and forth between us. His eyes darted away from me after only a second.

"No," Van said, giving me a look that was akin to a supportive hand on my shoulder, "Have you ever heard of a hostile work environment?"

"Yes." That careful tone in Marcus' voice had turned into something closer to the way people would approach a bomb.

And that was the appropriate way to approach him.

"Let's just say that working with him would be hostile to Andrew, if no one else," Van said, and I tried not to groan.

The last thing I wanted was have this part of the conversation with Marcus. Maybe I could go clean up the pepper with Zeda.

"What happened?" Marcus asked, but all hint that he was cautious was gone.

Now his voice was hard, and his fists clenched. It froze me in my chair, staring at him with my mouth slightly open. Not enough air got into my lungs.

"He does some distribution that we were trying to get our product into and..." Van looked over at me and bit her lip. "It just didn't work out. Unfortunately, he has a lot of pull in this world on the West Coast, and has made it hard for us since then."

I squeezed my eyes shut, trying not to remember that man's office, the phone calls, the perfectly chosen words so I was powerless to call him out.

There was a way out of this. I couldn't work with that guy. I just needed to find a way.

Opening my eyes again, I found Marcus staring at me. I couldn't tell what he was thinking, which only made my fear that much harder to hide. It wasn't just fear of that jerk and what would happen to Van's family, it was fear of what Marcus would think, that he would say screw this and be gone. Forever this time.

"Give me some time," he said, his voice almost hoarse, "but I'll try my best to help."

"Why did you agree to help again?" Ceecee asked over the speaker when I called her the next day on my way to work to tell her all about it.

"You didn't see his face," I said, waiting at the light, and trying to pay attention to the traffic instead of the image of him that flashed into my head. "He looked scared."

"But why is it suddenly your responsibility to save him? He wasn't there to save you."

She wasn't wrong. He left me without any mention of why, without an apology, with nothing.

"It isn't my responsibility, but it is my job to try."

Ceecee stopped arguing. But I heard her sigh, and tried not to let it get to me too much. I was already almost shaking about going into work today. Today was the day I would start focusing on trying to find some way to do what she thought I shouldn't even try to do. And that meant more time being around him.

"And?" she finally said, which made me shake my head and look at my phone in the holder as if it would make her make sense.

"And, what?" I asked.

"What's the other reason, Marcus?" she asked, and I choked on the air.

"Oh, look," I said, "almost at work."

"Don't do it. Don't you hang up on me. You know I'm right."

"Got to go, Ceecee."

"Not yet you don't. Tell me you aren't falling for him again."

"Should I tell you I'm over him?" I asked, the words tasting almost as bad in my mouth as the pepper did last night.

"Yes. You worked so hard for so long to get past him and what he did."

"Past, Ceecee," I said, my voice a whisper as I turned into the parking lot of the brewery, and actually looked at the sign.

"What do you mean, Marcus?" she asked.

"The name of the brewery is Mason Jar."

She sucked in a breath loud enough for it to echo through my speakers and surround me in my car as I parked.

"Do you think…"

"I don't know. I don't know what to think. But we both know that getting past isn't the same as getting over, and seeing him scared was…" I rubbed my hands over my face, and tried to make the thoughts roiling in my mind line up into something that I could figure out, something I could read instead of hieroglyphics.

"Fine," she said with an exaggerated exhalation that made a smile twitch on my face, "but if he makes you cry, he's going to be scared again, and I won't apologize."

"As long as you don't scare him with Theresa and her equipment," I said.

"Hey," Theresa yelled from somewhere in the background.

"Love you, Theresa, but you're not allowed to kill him." I laughed, and so did Ceecee.

"Someday," Theresa yelled from the background, "one of my friends will need my access to construction sites. I'm just going to keep offering it to all you people who are way too sweet, so when that person finds themselves in that situation, they know to call me."

"For a former cheerleader," I said, shaking my head, "you might be the scariest person I know."

"My work here is done," she said, and we all laughed.

"Thanks, guys. I really do have to go to work now."

"Love you," we all said, and I hung up, looking at the Mason Jar Brewery.

Did he name it after me? After my last name? And how would I ever find out if he did or not?

When I got hired, I thought it was just a cute name about the old canning jars people used back in the days of Prohibition to make their own alcohol. Now though…

I shook my head, and tried to focus on what I needed to do today.

Bringing my bag with me, with my water bottle, notebooks, and other necessities, I wondered if something would hit me that might actually help. Maybe I would just be one more person worrying about it, and unable to actually do anything that would matter.

Making my way inside, I wasn't surprised to find Vanessa and Shane already here, standing in the doorway of his office, talking about something.

"Hey, Marcus," Vanessa said, waving me over, "do you want to set up in my office today?"

"Um, hi, I…" had no idea how to answer that. Where was I supposed to be setting up and working through everything?

"It will be your office in three weeks anyway," she said, smiling. Shane looked down at the floor.

"Three weeks?" I asked, my voice coming out as a squeak. This was a lot tighter timeline than I was expecting.

"Don't worry," she said, putting a hand on my arm, "that's just my last day in Washington. Probably not my last at work."

Shane still wouldn't look up, his hand braced on the doorframe in a tight grip. He looked like he wanted to say something, but was holding himself back.

"Oh. Sure, as long as I'm not in your way, I'll work in there today." I wasn't sure how to respond to anything. One day I decided my path here, what I needed to do, and the next turned it all upside down again. Part of me was waiting for it to happen again.

"You won't be in my way. Plus, it will give you a place to run to if Zeda gets crazy with her ideas again."

"Pray for me," I said, groaning.

At that, Shane lifted his eyes to mine, pain slicing through me at the softness in them.

I turned around and fled after Vanessa, trying to put him out of my mind.

But her office was just on the other side of the walkway to the kitchen, and I couldn't help looking back toward Shane as I walked in behind her.

He was still looking at me, biting his lower lip.

While Shane's office was almost like a time warp back to some speakeasy with an antique desk and dark woods with rustic touches, this office was a modern and sleek, mostly clean slate with two boxes in the back corner.

"You would be surprised how much stuff I accumulated in my offices," Vanessa said, looking down at the boxes and tapping one with the toe of her boot. "These are the last of it, and I need to get them out of here."

She shook her head as she took a seat at the desk.

The desk was glass with a laptop open on one end, and a chair on each side of it, making it look more like a dining table everyone could gather around than a desk.

I liked it. It gave the room a vibe that there wasn't the same kind of boss dynamic happening in here.

Of course, I also liked how comfortable and cozy Shane's overstuffed office was. Or, I would have probably liked it if every second I spent in it wasn't overshadowed by the mess my brain was in his presence.

Vanessa gestured for me to take a seat, and I did, pulling out my notebooks.

"Behind you, on that shelf," she said, gesturing, "is a laptop for you to use. It's all set up, and there is a paper on how to install your passwords and everything."

"Thanks," I said, pulling down the paper and the computer from the otherwise empty white metal bookshelf behind me.

Part of me felt bad that I wasn't sure if this laptop would really end up being necessary. If I was only going to be here a little while, they would have to do all the work to reprogram it again.

Maybe it would be worth it if I could use the computer to help me make everything work out for them. Big maybe.

SHANE

He said, 'Pray for me.'

All day long, in the middle of doing something else, the thought would hit me again.

When he said it in jest and not at all in a way that invited the sentiment that ran through my mind, it was still hard for me not blurt out what I was thinking.

I always did.

That's what I wanted to tell him. I always prayed to the universe that he would be back in my life, that we would somehow have another chance.

Even when I was happy, when everything was going okay in the time since I left him, I still wanted him. He was what was missing.

But I wasn't allowed to think that way. He made it clear. He didn't want to hear anything I had to say about that.

So, I kept my mouth shut, and went about doing my job, trying to think up some way to make this right, to fix the problem we faced right now.

No matter how hard I tried, I couldn't keep out of my head all the ways I should have handled it differently back then. I couldn't stop my head from trying to solve that old problem instead.

That was probably why I found myself walking into Zeda's experiment room later, and coming face to face with Marcus.

He took my breath away when he looked up, his eyes crinkled in a smile.

I missed his smile so much, the way it shone from him, making it impossible not to smile along with him.

But before the answering grin formed on my own face, his smile fell away from his lips, and his eyes went back to guarded and careful.

"Hey, Boss," Zeda said, looking up at me and then back to Marcus, her face not showing any hint of what she thought. But I knew she didn't miss how we reacted to each other. There was little she missed.

"Z," I said, deciding it was better to act as normal as possible than it was to turn around and hide in my office again, "no more problems with pepper?"

She tilted her head at me, and didn't deign to respond to that. Instead, she said, "I'm almost done showing Marcus everything. Although, I don't know how much good it will do."

"What? Why?" I asked as Marcus rolled his eyes.

"It's not my fault I still don't entirely speak foodie," he said, "Lord knows I'm surrounded by them."

"Foodie?" I asked, unable to hide the grin sneaking onto my face.

"He keeps equating beer and the brewing process with something like what his friend does with her bakery." Zeda shook her head, and went back to making a note in her notebook.

"Just because you think it's vastly different," Marcus went on, smiling with his head high, and showing no sign he was going to back down from this, "doesn't mean that it actually is. You both talk about flavor profiles, and the way one ingredient needs to compliment another."

"Your friend may use similar words, but the processes are vastly different. And the whole notion that brewing and baking are similar in any way is just incorrect." Zeda didn't sound angry, but she did sound dumbfounded. I had to bite my lip to keep from laughing.

"This coming from someone who thought adding pepper to a beer would be a good idea," he said, and I lost control and laughed.

Zeda shot me a look that I knew meant I would hear about this later.

"Look out, Marcus," I said, and he froze, which made me almost stop talking. My voice going quiet, "You keep talking to her like that, and she'll claim you as a brother."

By the time I was done, they both stared at me, Marcus with a tight expression I hoped didn't hide pain, and Zeda with one brow raised.

She looked back and forth between us, and I hoped she had not mentioned that she already called me her brother, that the reason the words coming out of my mouth might have been that desperate wish still in me that one day he really would be family. My family.

"Well," Zeda said, wiping her hands on her pant legs, "Sunshine over here will have to be tough to be a brother of mine."

"Not that again," he whined, and I fought back tears that welled in the back of my throat.

"Again?" she asked, tilting her head.

He rubbed at a spot above his eyebrow.

"In high school they called me Sunny for some ridiculous reason," he said.

"They called you Sunny because you always managed to make everyone around you happy," I said, my voice low and mumbled, but he heard me.

Marcus looked at me and swallowed before casting his eyes back down to the floor.

"High school was a long time ago," he said, and a piece of my heart flaked off.

Did he mean it was too long ago? That *I* was too long ago?

Zeda looked back and forth between us before her eyes widened.

"You were Sunny and Shane," she said, and cracked up laughing.

"Okay," he said, throwing his hands in the air, "that's my cue to go. I'll talk to you later about my idea."

Marcus stomped out of the room, and I shook my head as Zeda looked at me, laughter still on her face.

"What did I say?" she asked.

"That's what they actually called us after we got together. They thought it was hilarious, and Marcus hated it because that meant he wasn't Cher." I shook my head, and let out a puff of breath.

She walked over to me, and leaned against the wall next to me, studying me as I trained all my attention on the floor.

"Have you talked to him yet?" she asked.

"No. I tried, but he doesn't want to." And I was afraid to try again, or have him really leave instead of just leaving the room.

"Boss," she said, planting a hand on my shoulder, "You need to talk to him. Tell him it's still him, and how pathetic you've been all these years."

"I haven't been pathetic." It was an automatic reaction, to try and defend myself. But I really had been in a lot of ways.

"When was your last date?" she asked.

"Um…" I assumed she meant the last date I went on period, and not the last date I had with him. "That time you tried to set me up with your chef friend."

"You went on one date and left early. The time before that,

we had to trick you to go with someone, and when you realized it was a date, you ran away."

Pressing my lips together, I remembered that night. My friends had made it sound like we were all going as a group to a show, one I really wanted to see. But I left during the intermission when the only people who showed were me and some guy that they thought I would like.

"In the years since you last saw him, you have gone on a grand total of two first dates, and neither of those were your idea. It's still him."

"Z, we both know, it will always be him." And even as I said it, it sunk in. That was the truth. Marcus was it for me, and always would be.

"Fate dropped him right into your path, and did it in such a way that he doesn't seem able to sprint as far and as fast from you as possible. Take the chance." She patted my shoulder, and went back to what she was doing while I tried to figure out what taking the chance would even look like.

And if I took that chance, if I held out a hand to him, would he take it?

What would I do if he didn't?

MARCUS

The end of the day on Sundays came earlier than the end of the day Fridays and Saturdays.

I texted Ceecee and Theresa to let them spread the word to the others in Theresa's group chat.

A vague idea was forming in my head, but I would need to run it by them before I said anything to Shane and Vanessa.

Not more than ten minutes later, Ceecee texted back that the group was all in, and we would meet at Joe's tomorrow for dinner.

"Perfect," I said, putting my phone back in my pocket.

"What's perfect?" Shane asked, coming up next to me. I almost fell over.

He was perfect. He always was. And it took a physical effort not to say it out loud.

"Some friends of mine are meeting me for dinner tomorrow. They just agreed to the plan."

"Ah. Right," he said, putting a hand on the back of his neck in a nervous gesture I remembered. "Your boyfriend must be missing you when you're working all weekend. Probably really different from the bakery."

I rolled my eyes. All those football players…

"No boyfriend. Those guys were just friends that go a little overboard when they're…" well, crap. I said too much. "…when they're celebrating me getting a new job."

Shane grinned, and then coughed into a fist, looking around me, but not at me.

"That first day, I thought for a while you were dating half the UW football team," he said, and I couldn't help laughing.

"Most of the team I hardly know. One of them happens to be a good friend of mine who is too pure for this world, and he decided to round up the team to support me. It didn't hurt that there was beer involved." I waved it away, and tried to laugh along with him. It really was incredibly sweet. But there was no point in keeping up the pretense that Deacon thought was such a good idea. Especially because the last people I knew of who pretended to date ended up together, and I wasn't ready for that.

"Do you think we should do something like that?" Shane asked, his brow furrowed.

"Something like what?" In my own jumbled thoughts about fake dates, I was completely lost, and a little scared by whatever he was suggesting.

"A sports thing." He looked around the tasting room that was decidedly not set up like a sports bar.

"Well," I said, trying not to laugh at how little he knew about sports. "Football season is over, this place isn't set up for it, and I really don't think a guy who doesn't know the difference between a linebacker and a line drive should have anything to do with a sports bar."

"Hey," he said, putting a hand to his chest feigning hurt, "I know the difference between those two things. I'm not totally helpless."

"Really? So, you had a brain transplant recently?" I asked, raising a brow.

Shane grinned, opening his mouth, but then his eyes grew haunted. He looked at the ground.

For a minute, I forgot. I talked to him like nothing happened between us, like nothing was broken beyond repair. But the look on his face reminded me, along with whatever ghost was causing it.

It was possible he learned a lot about sports in the years we spent apart. It was possible that more changed about him than I realized or ever thought would. It was entirely possible he wasn't the same person I was in love with, that the man I thought I would spend the rest of my life with no longer existed.

"Anyway," he said, long after the moment grew too long and too full of awkwardness, "sports are probably out, but have any brilliant ideas struck you yet?"

"There is one thing I'm still working on, but I have another idea that I need to talk to you and Zeda about."

"New beer?" he asked, a half-smile forming on his face.

"Sort of." I nodded toward the experiment room as he cocked his head in a question. But I didn't wait for his response or his questions. I just began to head toward Zeda. If she said it wouldn't work, then I would have to come up with something else entirely.

For now, it was only one of my plans, and I hoped it worked because I still didn't have any idea how likely the other was to pan out.

Opening the door to her experiment room, I held my breath and braced myself for some unholy attack on my nose again.

"You think she dropped some more pepper?" Shane asked from behind me as he grabbed the door to walk in after me. The feeling of his body so close to mine was just one more thing I had to physically brace myself for.

"I will have nightmares about it," I said, trying to act like I was lighthearted and normal, although I didn't think I succeeded.

"A trauma response to a smell?" He laughed, and I rolled my eyes.

He knew how bad the pepper thing was for me. It wasn't new, but if he thought I was only awkward because of that, then maybe it would cover for some of the probably strange reactions I had to being around him.

"Z," he called out and Zeda emerged from the other side of one of the machines, whizzing along on a spinny chair, with a sandwich in her hand and a bag of chips in her lap. "Is this a bad time?"

"No. I'm fine. But I'm going to keep eating." She took another bite, and looked at us like we were the entertainment accompanying her meal.

"Right. So, I have an idea," I said when they both looked to me expectantly.

"Already?" she asked, popping a chip in her mouth.

Maybe it was too soon. Maybe this was a terrible plan.

I looked back and forth between them, unsure if I should even say anything now.

"He's brilliant, Z. I'm sure it's a good idea," Shane said, and I choked on some air, looking up at the top of the machines in front of me just so I could avoid his eyes as I sent a prayer to whoever would listen that I wouldn't blush. He didn't deserve a blush.

"Okay, settle down," Zeda said, she took another bite and looked at me, "hit me. What's your big plan."

"Do you have enough room back here and enough capacity to run, say, thirty new batches for an event?" I asked.

She leaned back in her chair, her brow furrowed, and her eyes narrowed.

"Why? That's a lot." Her voice was harder and more skeptical than it had been the other times we spoke, and I still wasn't sure if this was going to work at all.

"Because I think it would be a good promotional opportunity to have the staff all design their own new beer. We can have the public do taste tests. We could even sell merch, make it a game-like atmosphere where people root for their favorites, and the announcement could be made at the end of it all at a big party."

Zeda didn't show any reaction at all to my suggestion. She just took another bite of her sandwich and chewed.

Looking over to Shane, his eyes were far away, and one corner of his mouth was quirked up in the way that said he was picturing something in his head.

"Vanessa's party," he said, turning to look at Zeda. "In three weeks, we could have all the merch and everything prepared while the batches brew. And then we can unveil them at Vanessa's going away party. Then we start the buzz for the tasting and voting period, which we'll say will last two weeks, and then we have a big party for the announcement of the winner."

"How exactly would this work for more than a temporary influx of revenue?" Zeda asked, continuing to eat her food as if we weren't talking about a huge amount of work for her and for everyone else.

"We say it will be an annual tradition, and every winning beer will be named after the year it was made and the person who made it, with a sub name they choose," I said, hoping she wasn't going to say it was far too much work.

"That sounds like a Taylor Swift album," she said.

"Yes," I said. "Exactly like that. We could turn the merch into things that play on that idea, album cover type images. I bet we could find local artists who would want to be part of it for a portion of the profit off the sale of the shirts and things. This is Seattle. We have a lot of artists. So, then they would probably promote their own to their friends and family, all the staff involved would, and the regulars."

"Okay," Zeda said, taking another bite, and looking over to the side, "long term, how does this continue to bring in more business."

"There's something else I'm working on, but I can't talk about it yet. For now, it would help to have more people know about us, and enjoy their time here. If this place becomes some-where people think to come, think to order from, and bring their friends to…if it becomes someone's favorite beer, all of that will help."

"Send the staff in right away. I am going to be pressed for time to get this all done." Zeda smiled, finally, and wheeled her chair away without another word.

"Did that go well, or…" I asked, looking at Shane who gave me his brightest smile, and almost knocked me over in the process.

"That went very well."

SHANE

For a minute he was there. After all this time, and all this tension since we saw each other again, for just a little bit today he was the Marcus I remembered while he was talking to me.

That first day, I saw the way he acted with his friends and other people, and he was exactly the same. But every time he was around me, he was different.

I understood. I was different, too. So much happened, and I screwed up so badly that I expected worse.

But today, he was there, with the jokes and the grins. Every piece of the fun Sunny version of Marcus was in front of me, even if there was still a distance.

More than his idea, and the stream of employees that went to see Zeda, it was seeing the old Marcus that had me floating through the rest of the day.

Every time I looked at him, while he was working and I was on the other side of the room, I stopped and stared for a minute, smiling like an idiot.

He caught me more than once, and I had to remind myself to get moving again.

It was just so hard not to.

"Andrew," Vanessa said at one point when I did it right in front of her in mid-sentence and Marcus caught me, turning away as fast as he could, "you need to stop that. He's going to run if you don't figure out how to stop doing that."

"Yeah, Van," I said, grabbing the back of my neck, and looking down at the floor so I could school my face, "I know, it's just…"

"That you're getting your hopes up."

"I…" Was I? Was I being ridiculous? Was I starting to think I might have a chance at getting him back?

"No," I said, all chance of smiling like a fool well and truly gone again, "I don't expect him to forgive me and take me back. He…"

Pressure built behind my eyes, and my throat closed up as I realized that I was actually getting my hopes up, and that it would never happen.

"Even if he forgave me enough to work with me long term, and even if he forgave me enough to be friends one day, I can't see him ever trusting me enough for anything else." And that was the truth. I couldn't see that happening. Ever.

"Listen," she said, putting a hand on my arm, "I know this is hard, but maybe this is exactly what you need. Maybe now you can move on, too."

Too. She said move on, too, like she thought he had moved on from me. Maybe he had. All he said was that he didn't have a boyfriend right now. That didn't mean there wasn't a boyfriend since me.

"Yeah," I said instead of anything else running through my brain, "maybe."

She smiled at me, patted my arm, and walked away.

I looked back to Marcus, and watched as he chatted and laughed with one of the bartenders.

He was every bit my Marcus, my Sunny, spreading his light to every person around him.

But he wasn't mine anymore. And he would never be again.

No matter how much I wanted to be back in that place with him where he could shine all day and I got to watch, knowing I got to soak up his warmth, and feed every bit of light I had in me back to him when we were alone.

The pride of knowing I got to see him through the moments when the darkness got him, too, was enough to get me through the worst moments of my life. It was enough for me to believe I had more worth than I had thought before we met.

It was probably normal for someone like me to want everything he was back in my life. It was probably normal for me to get my hopes up that I could get him through the dark again.

Even as he looked up and met my eyes, no smile forming on my face this time, I knew that I was fooling myself. Van was right.

People like me didn't get that lucky twice.

His eyes were still on me when I looked away, and went back to focusing on what I was doing.

"Do you have the list ready?" Vanessa asked sometime later when I had been so into what I was doing that I missed the tasting room closing for the night.

"Yeah," I said, going to my office, and getting the lists I made for people to sign up with their artist contact information, including one where they could name artists that other people could try out.

"Wait," Marcus said, running over to us. The way his ridiculously perfect hair moved with him as his body moved made my heart thump harder in my chest. "Don't forget to put on the list that you need to approve the art."

"I can't," I said, shaking my head, and reeling back from the list like they would bite me. The last thing anyone needed me doing was anything involving art.

"Shane," he said, his voice soft and sighing. It made me freeze and stare at him with the same pressure from earlier building behind my eyes. That was his voice he reserved for when he told me I was worth more than I thought. "You or Vanessa need to approve the art to protect the business."

"But I can't do it," I said again, my voice devoid of all emotion, so I didn't give anything away.

"You know you have better taste than you think." He raised his brows at me in that encouraging way he used to, and I could barely breathe.

"I shouldn't do it, either," Van said. "I'm not even sure if I would have enough time to do all of it on top of what I need to get done before I go."

"Shane's going to do it," Marcus said, smiling at me with a nod.

"Only if you help," I said, my voice low and barely more than a whisper. Fear of what he would say warred with my desperation to have his support and approval on this.

"This is your business. This should be up to you." He shook his head, but Van grinned and nodded, liking the idea.

"Well, I think it would be great for there to be two votes on all of the ideas," Van said. "And if you have an argument over one of them, then I'll be the tie breaker."

She smiled and walked away as if that was the end of the discussion, and there was no point in arguing.

"I guess that's the way she wants it," he said.

Looking back at him, I didn't see rage like I expected. I saw careful consideration and trepidation.

"Marcus," I said, and he flinched, "If this is…um…too…well, if you don't want to, I can try on my own."

"This is my job," he said, and I let out a breath, my shoulders releasing some of their tension as he turned around like was going to walk away. But, a second later, he whirled back toward me and set his jaw.

Holding myself as still as possible, I tried to brace my body and my heart for whatever he was about to say.

"Just stop saying my name that way," he said, and he walked away.

"Okay," I mumbled, although I didn't understand how he thought I was saying his name. Maybe I just needed to call him something else entirely.

MARCUS

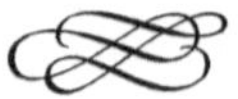

I never thought I would be so relieved to see the sign for Joe's pizzeria.

When Theresa's friends absorbed me and Ceecee into their circle, I wasn't expecting it to come along with regular nights eating at Joe's, the occasional trip to karaoke, and far too many nights shooting pool at The Shark, Campbell's new pool hall. But we gathered at each other's businesses far more often than we gathered at each other's houses.

If someone had a problem, we met up wherever worked for all of us. Part of me wondered if we weren't the oddest bunch of people on the planet.

The core group was two couples and three vagabonds, me being one of the vagabonds. Campbell and Olivia, and Ceecee and Theresa were all so perfect together in their relationships that it should have made Deacon, his cousin Katie, and I jealous. But I was just happy for them, and it seemed to be true for Deacon and Katie, too.

Of course, every once and a while, Omar, Campbell's cousin, came to a group event, too. Only then did the dynamic ever get weird, and that was only ever true when he and Katie both brought dates.

At some point, I was told, they were together. And even though they broke up and got along, they still got snippy when they both had dates around. If it was just one, everything was fine. But for some reason when they both did things could get tense.

Maybe I should have asked if Katie and Omar were going to come and bring dates.

But as I parked in the lot and got out of my car, I couldn't care too much.

This place, these people, along with Ceecee, had become a kind of medicine for me that kept me from succumbing to the worst things life had to offer.

If something bad happened to one of us, the others were there to pick them up.

For tonight, they didn't know it yet, but they might be able to help me more than just with their emotional support. Although I needed that, too.

Especially after today.

Just like the first two days of working with Shane, today turned me upside down, and left me reeling.

But now, I was at Joe's.

Opening the front door, the few people still sitting inside an hour before closing on a Sunday were so much quieter than the people in the tasting room. I took a deep breath. It tasted of pizza and comfort and all the best parts of my life.

"Marcus," Ceecee called, waving me over to the alcove table everyone liked to sit at.

A second later, on my way to the alcove, Campbell came around the corner with a pizza, and smiled at me.

"Hey, Marcus," he said as he dropped off the pizza, and went to help one of the other tables.

I waved at him and made my way to our other friends.

Ceecee was the first to reach me, enveloping me in a hug. She smelled of cinnamon rolls and freshly baked bread.

"Are you okay?" she asked.

"Yeah, I'm fine," I said, loud enough for all of them to hear me.

"Good," Theresa said, scooting out of the booth, too, and giving me a hug right after her girlfriend, "because I would have been disappointed if you called all these people here to tell me you need my heavy equipment."

"Theresa," Olivia said, coming from the back as well and giving me a hug, "we all love you, but you are mildly terrifying right now."

Olivia leaned over to Theresa and whisper-yelled, "And we have other people in the restaurant."

"None of them believe me," Theresa whisper-yelled back, a wild smile on her face.

"More than mildly terrifying, I think," I said as I slid into the booth.

"Deacon and Katie are on their way," Olivia said, "and as soon as Campbell has a chance, he'll come over, too. He's flipping the sign now."

"But I thought you all were open for another hour," I said.

Olivia looked over toward where Campbell was cashing out a bill and a soft smile formed on her face, her eyes may as well have been shaped like hearts. It made me smile.

"We've decided to start closing a little earlier on Sundays, and change some other hours so we can spend more time together."

"Couples goals," I said.

Theresa and Ceecee laughed, nodding because we all said it all the time. Olivia blushed.

"Anyone want to update their bets?" I asked, leaning back and crossing my arms while I grinned, and Olivia swatted at my arm, her blush getting worse.

Before Theresa and Ceecee could answer, Campbell popped up out of nowhere to kiss Olivia's cheek, and whisper something in her ear that made her bite her bottom lip.

He put a hand to the back of her neck, and pulled her in for a quick kiss, a wicked grin on his face.

"Keep making her blush and I'll owe you," he said, turning to me to slap me on the shoulder before he darted away again to keep working.

"Oh, really?" I asked.

"Yeah," Theresa said, shaking her head, and looking out toward Campbell, "I need to update my bet."

"What bet?" Olivia asked, ducking her head to hide the blush from the rest of the restaurant, and, therefore, Campbell.

"No one told her?" I asked, looking back and forth between a confused looking Theresa and a chagrined Ceecee.

"Told who, what?" Deacon asked, slapping me on the shoulder and shoving me over to make room for him.

Katie slipped under his big arm, and scooted into my side, wrapping an arm around me as she looked up at her cousin with the fakest version of an innocent smile on her face as she batted her lashes.

"Come on," Deacon said, "I never get to sit in the booth. I always have to sit in the chair."

"You can sit in the booth," Olivia said, "Campbell can sit in the chair."

"Olivia, the couples sit together," Deacon said, looking unamused that she would suggest anything else.

"Then Olivia will sit on his lap," Katie said, wiggling her eyebrows.

"Guys." Olivia widened her eyes, and her blush came raging back.

Campbell reappeared making a humming noise, and muttering something about killing him before he ran off again.

I just shook my head.

"Everyone is going to have to update their bets," Theresa said, leaning into Ceecee.

"Not me," Deacon said, "I already lost."

"What bets?" Olivia asked again.

"How did you already lose?" I asked, pulling out my phone, and looking up the list of bets we all had recorded there. "Really, Deek?"

"Yeah. I thought for sure they would be engaged two days after they moved in together."

"Wait, what?" Olivia screeched.

It took a little while for her to get over the shock that all her friends had taken bets on when she and Campbell would get engaged, but by the time the last customers left and he joined us, she just said, "Every last one of you will pay for that."

But then she got out of the booth and sat on Campbell's lap, whispering in his ear as he rubbed a hand up and down her back.

He grinned, looking over her shoulder at us, and gave us a thumbs up with the hand on her back that she couldn't see.

All of us did some version of stifling the laughter that wanted to spill out.

Deacon slapped both hands over his mouth, and squeezed his eyes shut.

Ceecee and Theresa buried their faces in each other's shoulders.

I buried mine in Ceecee's other shoulder, and Katie bit the side of her hand as she leaned on me.

When Olivia's blushing face popped up, Campbell saved us all by taking her chin and planting his lips on hers.

The move gave us enough time to recover, but it was a close thing.

"Okay," Olivia said, a little breathless as she settled into his arms and everyone started to grab their slices of pizza, "so, if everything is okay, then what's up, Marcus?"

"First," I said around a bite, "I want to thank all of you for helping me in this. I know I wouldn't have been able to get through that first day without you."

I looked around to all of them, even the ones that weren't there inside the brewery with me, because they were all part of the planning and all of them were there with me in spirit.

"Second," I said, wiping my mouth and putting down my pizza to lean back in my seat, "I think I need your help again."

SHANE

I paced back and forth behind my desk, Van sat in one of the chairs, and I tried not to let my hands shake.

"Why? I don't get why he has to come here?"

"He said he was already in Seattle for a meeting."

"But to just spring this on us?" I stopped and looked at Van, putting a hand to the back of my neck. "Why didn't you tell him no?"

"Andrew," she said, her voice cold.

"Fine," I said, because I knew why. That manipulative piece of crap had bought the bank we had our business loan through, and we couldn't risk him messing with it in retaliation. "But this can't happen all the time. I can't..."

The sound of footsteps through the tasting room carried around the mostly open door of my office, and Van and I exchanged wide eyed stares.

"Did he let himself in?" I whisper-shouted.

"I don't know. Didn't you lock the door?" she whisper-shouted back, springing to her feet.

She was out of my office first. My hands in fists, I rounded the door to watch as the stiff posture of her shoulders relaxed.

"Oh," she said, "hi, Marcus."

My fists unclenched, and I rushed out to see him. Being able to see him might help me get through this meeting.

Even without him knowing it, he was Sunny, and I needed his light right now.

"Hi, Vanessa," he said as I came to stand beside her. "Hi, Shane."

"You're here early," I said, when what I meant was, please never leave.

"Well," he said, standing a little straighter and smiling, one of those light giving displays that made him so beautiful I had trouble thinking, "I have some good news."

A knock sounded on the door and to me it was like the tolling of the bells of doom.

"Hold that thought," Van said, taking a deep breath, running her hands down the front of her skirt. She straightened her back, and stomped toward the front door.

Marcus furrowed his brow, watched her, and then looked me up and down.

No doubt he saw the way that every step she took toward opening the door made me tenser.

I expected him to leave, to flee to the safety of his office, leaving me with just the memory of his smile to see me through this.

Instead, he took a few steps closer to me, and turned toward the door, angling himself so he was between me and the door.

Taking a deep breath, I stood up straighter, and tried to pretend it meant what it would in a perfect world.

"Vanessa," the smarmiest voice in the world came from the door, the "s" elongated. It sent a shudder through me.

Marcus sucked in a hissing breath.

Even the greeting was enough to set off all his alarm bells.

"Hello, Walter," Vanessa said, her voice a monotone devoid of all emotion.

"Is your husband with you today? I so want to meet the lucky man who gets to take you home at night."

"So sorry, Walter, he isn't here."

Marcus turned to look at me with wide eyes.

"Yep," I muttered.

That was the thing about Walter, he said things that made you want to jump out of a window to get away from him, but they weren't gross enough to be actionable.

And he was an equal opportunity sleaze. He said things to everyone. Gay, straight, trans, cis, nonbinary. Literally anyone and everyone was fair game for his terrible attentions. And no one knew what he would actually do given the opportunity, what his preference actually was, or if he even had one. We saw him with the staff one night when he came to the tasting room in California. I finally had to step in and take care of his group on my own to protect them. But Van and I both knew that anyone who didn't have a partner were his favorite targets.

Van led Walter toward us. An older man with his dapper suit and hair dyed so only his sides were gray, he should have been fun to look at. But this man made me want to vomit and punch something.

"Andrew, my favorite," he said, with a shrug of his shoulder and a coquettish little smile that even made the word 'coquettish' unappetizing.

"Hello, Walter," I said, trying to keep my voice as neutral as his.

Then he spotted Marcus.

Eyes widening, mouth opening, he made no secret of the way he dragged his gaze over Marcus' body, and a shiver of excitement went through him that made me want to tuck Marcus behind my back.

"Who is this beautiful friend? Did you all hire someone new?" Walter's voice was lower, more calculating, and, if it was possible, made me even more sure that we were dealing with a predator.

"No, of course not," Marcus said in a sultry purr before Van or I could say anything.

Van blinked, and I tried to figure out what I should do and what game Marcus was playing right now. Meanwhile, Walter almost vibrated with barely-constrained glee.

Marcus stepped back and wrapped himself around my arm, leaning into me, and threading his fingers with mine.

Any other time, having him touch me like this would send all my senses into overdrive, but I was already deep into preparing to fight as my fight or flight was triggered. So instead, I just clung onto his hand, and tried to act natural.

"I'm Marcus, and I just came to spend the day with the love of my life," Marcus said, his voice still just dripping with sex appeal, and yet terrifyingly threatening at the same time. "I'm so happy he moved here to be with me after all. And, what a bonus, I finally get to meet the famous Walter."

The way he said 'Walter' was as if he was putting out a hit on the man by saying his name.

Van's eyes were wide, but she was just as frozen as I was.

With every word out of Marcus' mouth, every caress of my arm, Walter's slimy smile shifted further toward pursed lips with a curl of the upper lip that suggested he smelled something bad. His eyes grew more tired.

"Love of your life?" Walter sounded livid. "I didn't know you were dating anyone, Andrew."

"I've known Andrew since we were children." Marcus said "known" as if it meant so much more. I swallowed, trying to keep up.

But there was probably no hiding the way I looked at him curled around me. We had known each other since we were kids. Even if this was a game, he was the love of my life. And I so wanted this to be real.

"My love," Marcus said, turning to look at me. He ran a hand along my chest, and I caught it with my free hand. My heart flew faster than it had in years. He blinked and almost lost it, but I smiled to encourage him. "Did you not tell your friends about me?"

His voice was a whisper, and didn't perfectly match the pout on his face. It made me drop my hand back to my side, knowing that what I was about to say mattered even though he was rubbing that hand along my chest again and still playing the game.

"I just want you all to myself," I said.

Finally, Marcus stopped, smiled and went back to cuddling my arm.

Walter looked at his watch.

"Oh, what a shame," Walter said, his voice sounding like a normal businessman. It took physical effort not to drop my jaw. "I forgot about a meeting I must get to. I'll see you all. It was nice to meet you, Marcus."

He turned on his heel and stalked out, the door shutting behind him.

Marcus stepped back from me, and smiled like an innocent child as Van and I stared at him.

"What on Earth was that?" Van asked while I just gaped like a fish on a line, wanting to pull him back, and knowing I couldn't.

"I'm assuming that's the guy you were talking about?" he asked.

Van and I both nodded.

"You warned me what he was like," Marcus said, "and I took the chance that someone who enjoyed pushing boundaries would be put off if someone staked one in the same gross way."

Without a single thought about the possible repercussions, or what he would say, just on the desperate urge and automatic response to him saving me, I grabbed him in a hug. One that meant something real this time.

"Thank you," I said, and let him go, stepping back.

But even as I looked at him, at the rapid blinking and the blank stare, I felt every single inch of my body that he touched in our hug.

Including where his hands grasped at my sides.

MARCUS

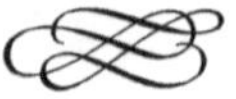

Code red. I screwed up. I skipped all the yellow, lit myself on fire, and just jumped into the red-hot disaster end of a vat of oil with all my clothes on.

What was I thinking?

Shane didn't need me to save him. Even if that guy made my skin crawl and some twisted, left-over protectiveness reared its ugly head, I should have been able to stop myself from crawling all over Shane.

I even called him Andrew.

Code red.

Maybe I skipped right over red, and landed in some fuchsia or purple.

How was I supposed to act around him now?

And he hugged me. He thanked me.

Run away, Marcus. Just run as fast as you can.

"Seriously, thank you Marcus," Vanessa said, and I nodded out of habit, my entire body tearing along the lines where I touched him, the rest of me so angry it was left out that I was ripping in two.

"Um…" I muttered, crossing my arms, and hugging my sides.

In a merciful world, I would think of a reason to leave. In a just world, I could walk out and never have to face Shane or what I just did again.

But this was a cruel world, and it wanted to kill me.

"What did you want to tell us?" Vanessa asked while Shane just stood there staring at me. I begged the world to open a hole and swallow me.

"Oh." I shook my head, trying to focus on Vanessa, but I felt Shane's gaze on me. Apparently, my mouth was broken, and could only speak in monosyllabic, unhelpful half words.

"Maybe we all need to go sit down," Vanessa said, looking back and forth between Shane and me, seeming increasingly unsure of what was going on.

But how was I supposed to help her figure it out when I didn't know either?

I followed along after her, my legs not feeling like they were connected to the rest of me the right way.

That made sense, though. My legs didn't rub up against Shane and get flooded with memories of the days I was allowed to touch him, and he was allowed to touch me.

We went into the office I shared with Vanessa, and sat around the table.

Looking down at my hands through the shining glass surface of the table, clutched tightly together in my lap, I took a deep breath.

Vanessa put a bottle of water in front of me and one in front of Shane. Then she pulled a box of donuts from somewhere behind her. The logo wasn't one I recognized.

"You know," I said, gesturing to the box, still refusing to meet Shane's eyes, "the best place to get treats in the morning is The Bake Place. Amazing cinnamon rolls." Baked goods were one of the few things I was certain I could talk about no matter the circumstances

"That's where you used to work, right?" Vanessa said, grabbing one and taking a bite.

She would recognize it; she did my interview, and she was probably the one to call Ceecee about my reference.

"Yeah," Shane said, taking a donut, too, his voice tight and thin, "Ceecee, the owner, is good people."

At that, even though I didn't want to do it, my eyes snapped up to look at Shane.

He was mid-bite, and paused before continuing, looking down at the donut in his hand.

"Next time I pick something up, I'll check it out," Vanessa said.

I nodded and took a deep breath, trying to put myself back on track.

With the shaking of my hand contained by sheer force of will, I grabbed my water bottle and took a drink.

"Ceecee is part of what I need to talk to you about, actually."

Taking a peek at both of them, I made sure they were listening, and barreled on with what I wanted to say.

"Between Ceecee, Olivia, Campbell, and some others I know, we already have at least six restaurants that have agreed to work out a distribution deal with us."

"Six?" Shane blurted, grin wide.

"Wait, really?" Vanessa said with a chirp as she dropped her donut to scramble for a notepad and pen.

"Yeah. Here," I said, pulling the list out of my back pocket. "Around here, and the rest of the state, there are a lot of businesses with liquor licenses that we could approach to carry our beer."

"How did you approach these?" Vanessa said, looking over the list.

"I called my friends, and they started calling theirs. They'll continue to give me leads, and asked their friends to do the same. I'm going one by one, and via personal connection. None of the big names have that."

"Exactly how many friends do you have that have some kind of restaurant connection?" Vanessa asked, eyes wide.

"You would be surprised," I said, laughing to myself. "Most of my friends have some connection to foodie things. And their connections have even more connections in that world."

"Didn't I say you weren't expected to save the day in the first week?" Shane asked, smiling at me in a way that made me feel like I was his even though I wasn't.

"Well," I said, trying to focus on what we were really talking about, "don't get too excited. It's a lot of work to organize, to deliver, and we can only hope that more businesses sign up. Only six won't fix things."

"You already helped with Walter today, and this is a start. Let's cross our fingers it gets things moving," Vanessa said, chewing her bottom lip.

"I'll keep working on it," I said, not wanting her to continue to stress in the same way.

"Marcus, I know," she said, with a smile as she pushed herself to her feet, "and so are we. I have a few phone calls to make."

She pulled out her cell phone and left the office, leaving me alone with Shane.

He stared at me and the air thinned, as if he was taking it all in. I had the feeling he was going to say something, maybe start a conversation I wasn't ready to have.

"Zeda," I blurted, jumping to my feet. "I need to check with her on how many people have worked out their beers with her."

I made my way around the table, trying to hide my deep breaths.

"You should do one, too," Shane said, stealing any veneer of calm I had with just his voice.

"What?" I asked, truly wondering what he said, and just as scared that it was something that mattered.

"This is your idea. You should create a beer, too. Talk to Zeda about it." His voice was soft, and there was an uncharacteristic waver in it that made me want to run even more.

Speaking was out of the question, if I opened my mouth, I probably would have word-vomited some nonsensical gobbledygook all over him.

Instead, I nodded, turned around again, and fled as fast as I could without breaking into an all-out sprint.

Hopefully, I could work through the day without seeing him again, let alone talking to him. And I definitely needed to avoid touching him again.

Even as I made the promise to myself to avoid him, my hands shook at my sides, wanting to thread his fingers into mine.

*M*arcus avoided me for the next two weeks.

At first, I thought it was just my paranoid concern over everything that happened when Walter showed up. Until Van said something about it.

"Has Marcus even spoken to you?" she asked when we walked into the break room to check on the lists, and he almost ran out of there.

"No. And I…" I stared at the door he just slipped out of. The image of his back filled my mind, and I didn't know what to say. It wasn't like I had a plan to deal with this, so I admitted, "I don't know what to do."

"You need to talk to him. This can't just go on this way. I will be leaving in a matter of days, and I need to know you two can have a conversation." She rubbed two fingers along her cheek, right next to her ear.

"Sorry for giving you a headache," I said.

"Really, I'm fine. This isn't all you." She put an emphasis on "all," and a small smile crept onto my face.

"Van, is there anything I can do?" I knew her kids, her husband, and his mom were probably all among the things weighing on her. And I also knew I was not likely to be able to help much in that regard. But I always asked. Maybe one day I could actually be of use to her outside of the brewery.

Pausing, she looked at me, her head cocked, and her eyes assessing.

"You know what?" she asked, and, suddenly, I regretted offering.

There was no telling what she was about to ask me to do, and I owed Van way too much to tell her no.

She let the silence between us build, let me fidget uncomfortably as I waited for her to hand down my punishment for whatever she thought I did wrong.

"Is this what growing up with you would have been like?" I asked, rubbing a hand along the back of my neck.

Her lips pressed into a line.

"Personally, I see no sign that you have grown up."

Dropping my hand to my side, my jaw followed, falling open.

"Wait, what?"

Van sighed and put a hand on my arm.

"Listen, Andrew, I know you're trying to make this work for me, and you're trying to make it happen as fast as you can. But we need to talk about a backup plan."

I swallowed. I didn't want to talk about a backup plan.

Sweat started in the small of my back.

"Okay," I said, looking around the break room at the few people around a table at the other end who were playing a card game, laughing, and paying zero attention to us. "Not here, though."

Van nodded and we grabbed our lunches, heading out toward my office.

The last time we had a discussion about backup plans she brought up the additional partner thing that sent us on the path that led to Walter visiting with disturbing regularity.

Making our way to the office, I scanned the tasting room, trying to soak up all the ways this brewery had gone right before Van reminded me of the challenges. My eyes landed on Marcus as he laughed at something a woman said while she grinned at him.

Why was I so against taking on another partner? Because the truth was, even without Walter's interference, I didn't want anyone else to be involved in this place.

I stopped walking, watching as Marcus spread that bright smile all through the room to everyone who had the good fortune to be near him.

And I figured out why I didn't want anyone else involved, why this meeting in my office made me sweat and weakened my legs.

Because I was afraid that I would have to tell Van the truth. And more than that, that she would resent me for it.

Marcus looked up, and his eyes met mine.

Without worrying about how he would take it, or the fact that he avoided me like it was part of his job requirement, I smiled at him.

He paused, as if he was shocked, as if smiles from me were a strange occurrence.

Averting his gaze, he looked at the floor, and his hand fluttered up to touch his mouth as one corner of his lips curled up. He darted in the other direction.

I made him smile.

Even if he fought it, even if he was so unsure of me that he avoided me, he smiled back.

That was a start.

Finally, I began heading to my office again, bracing myself for whatever was about to happen. Marcus and his little grin fueled me.

When I sat down at my desk, Van was already pulling out

her lunch, and I followed suit. Tension built in the silence between us.

"Can I tell you what I think without it being a problem?" she asked, startling me enough to almost drop my sandwich. She was still putting cream cheese on her bagel.

"Sure, go ahead," I said, although my brain screamed no.

"I think you need to take on partners, or get a loan. I don't know if there will be enough time to have all these new things raise enough revenue."

To stall, I took a bite too big for my mouth.

"We've gone down the partner route," I reminded her, trying not to make this about my own reticence.

"But with Walter out of the way..."

"Are you sure he is? Or is he just biding his time?" That was crappy of me. It could have been true that he was waiting in the wings to mess things up again, but I wasn't about to try and find out. I didn't want some unknown partner in the business.

She looked down at her bagel, her face twisting up to the side as she thought.

"Tell me the truth, Andrew. Why don't you want a partner? Even before Walter threw a wrench in things, when we were first starting, we mortgaged everything, and killed ourselves making it work when getting one would have been the much easier course."

It would have been. That was true. And if we had taken on a partner, it wouldn't be so hard for me to buy her out now. She would have been in an easier financial position.

"Because I don't want some stranger coming in here and wanting to change everything. This place is..." What? What was it about this place, this *business* that felt so personal?

"Have you told him?" she asked, making me snap my eyes to meet her gaze. "You won't talk to him. But it's right there, Andrew. The sign says Mason Jar Brewery, and you've made this whole business your baby. He needs to know."

"There are other reasons why I don't want to bring in some stranger. It isn't just the name." But even I didn't entirely believe my own words.

"Whatever happens, however we make this work, he should know for sure. He should know about why you left the way you did. Otherwise, you're just taking away his choice in the matter all over again."

My sandwich sat forgotten even as I squeezed it too tight in my hands.

"How, Van? How do I even start that conversation?" My voice was a weak pretense of what it normally was, but it told the truth. I was too weak to try and have that conversation again after he made it clear he didn't want to hear it last time I tried.

"You just begin. How did you start that letter you wrote him?"

"I told him I loved him. But..." I dropped my sandwich, and rubbed my hand over my face, "what do I do if he rejects me, if he doesn't want me?"

"The same thing you did when you were without him before."

"Cry?"

She nodded, her smile soft, "Cry on my shoulder. But at least you would know. And maybe you wouldn't be trying to hold on to the dream so tightly that you strangle it in the process."

MARCUS

"**A**re you sure this will work as a beer?" I asked Zeda, looking over her shoulder as she wrote notes down about tweaks that I wanted to the beer we started.

"There are some infused with all kinds of fruit," she said, making a mark of some formula I didn't understand even after hovering over her and this room more times than I had any right to. "The summer ales are almost always tinged with citrus, usually orange, but this is the same idea."

"Okay." I wanted to ask her opinion on the name, too. But that was going too far. She still called it my brew. I didn't want to put her in the position of knowing more, and feeling pressured to keep it to herself.

"Have you picked a name yet?" she asked, continuing to ignore my physical presence just over her shoulder as if she was the only person in the world it didn't bother to have someone so close.

"I'm working on it," I said, trying to ignore the tingle that went through me when she made it seem like she was reading my mind.

She made a humming noise, and didn't press the issue.

"All the other brews are on track as well?" I asked, pretending to have a reason to be in here beside my nerves over doing this for my brew.

"Yes. Just like the last time you asked."

I laughed, although she didn't say it with any hint of humor in her voice.

Zeda whirled around in her spinny chair, her gaze flat as she stared at me.

"Marcus, I say this with love."

Nothing about her voice said love, and I braced myself for whatever she was about to say.

"You need to talk to the boss, and you need to get out of my hair."

Shoulders dropping because she was kicking me out, it took a second for the rest of her statement to register in my head. Then my shoulders went right back to stiff and held too high.

"What are you talking about?" Smooth.

My voice was a weird squeak—the height of subtlety—which did nothing to make her think she got to me.

Yeah, right.

Zeda crossed her arms and stared at me with no sign that she was even willing to play along with my inane attempt to pretend I didn't know what she was talking about.

"The boss is being stupid. He's in here all the time to check on everything. When he's not in here, you're in here. Meanwhile, we are days away from Vanessa leaving this place for good, and last I checked, no one has managed to find a way to buy her out."

"Why do you call him the boss, and her Vanessa?" I asked, trying not to think about anything else she was saying.

"Because this was only ever a good investment for Vanessa. This was always his baby. Well, his and mine."

"You've been with him from the start?"

"Of course. I was his moms' next-door neighbor when he

moved down. Before he got there, I was taking care of her as much as I could. Before I even met Vanessa, he and I were friends."

"His mom?" I asked, something in her story making ice run through my veins like my body heard more than my brain did.

Zeda narrowed her eyes and cocked her head.

"Do you not know?" Nothing in her voice said she was surprised. The look on her face and her words suggested she was, and it made me wonder for the thousandth time how much anyone in Shane's life knew.

"The only thing I know is that he left me without a word one day, and all our friends lied for him, telling me they had no idea why he moved, where he went. And didn't know it was coming."

"But he left you a letter." She shook her head, the narrowed eyes widening now.

"No. I never got a letter. If he told you that it was a lie."

"Marcus, I swear, he left you a letter. He still didn't tell you the whole truth, but there was a letter."

I swallowed. I could ask the question and finally know, or I could stay in this place where maybe my heart wouldn't have to be broken again. Because how could the truth not break my heart anew?

"Whatever took him away, it was more important than me, or telling me the truth." I took a deep breath and met her eyes, not sure if I should admit my own truth to her now. "I'm not sure I want to know what could be that important to him."

"That's fair," she said, whirling back around to her note-books and computers.

She took away any reason for me to continue to hang out in there, so I turned and headed around the machines toward the door.

But Shane came around the corner, too, and I almost ran right into him.

"Hi," he said, his voice low and sweet.

I couldn't say anything back, I just nodded. My mouth wouldn't move, not after what Zeda said.

Putting a hand to the back of his neck, he looked at the floor.

"Did you really leave a letter?" I blurted, and slapped a hand over my mouth.

Everything in him seemed to pause.

Shane stepped back with one foot, his body rigid as if he was bracing himself.

"You didn't get my letter?" he asked, his voice low and barely a whisper.

"No. You just disappeared without a word." My voice was as hushed as his, and muffled by my shaking hands in front of my face.

"I put it in the book you were reading. The one on your nightstand so you would be sure to see it, and it wouldn't fall under the bed like your card." He shook his head, a breath whooshing out of him, his eyes brightening as he took a step toward me and reached out a hand.

Just as his fingers touched mine, the lightest brush of his skin, he said, "Marcus."

Darting around him, a sob wrenching from my throat, drowned by my hands over my face, I ran for the door.

He said it the way he always used to, as if he was saying he loved me, but I had to know if that was true or not. I needed to know.

"Marcus," he called after me, but I didn't stop. Even after I was in the tasting room, people all around, I didn't slow or pause to think about anything.

Running out of the brewery and to my car, I got the door open without even seeing the keys in my hands.

Tears streamed down my face as I fled the parking lot to get home as fast as I could.

Did he leave me a letter? Did he tell me what was going on? Was there contact information on it? Did I actually leave him?

Did I make him think all these years that I didn't love him, and once he was out of sight he was out of mind?

It didn't take me long to get home. If someone paid me to tell them about the drive, I wouldn't have been able to.

My mind was stuck back in my dorm, on the book I couldn't bring myself to pick up again because he said he wanted to borrow it when I was done.

Scrambling into my apartment, not sure what I was thinking other than an urgent need to know the truth that rivaled the need for oxygen in my lungs, my phone rang in my pocket.

I didn't answer it.

No matter who was on the other end of the call, I wouldn't have been able to form a coherent sentence.

All the way at the back of my closet, covered in dust, under boxes of things I rarely ever touched like my sleeping bag, I found the blue plastic tote that had everything from our life together closed up inside it.

Everything I didn't want to see again after he was gone went into the tote.

Now it held more than memories of perfection and pain.

It might hold the truth. And if it did, that might be my future.

After getting here, to the moment of opening it as fast as I possibly could, looking at the tote, my hands on the lid, I froze.

My phone rang again, and I ignored it.

The notification of text messages started going off and kept going.

But I couldn't move.

Not to open the tote, not to answer the phone, not even to chuck it across my room to get it to shut up.

All I could do was stare at the tote in front of me, hands shaking, breath shallow, and hope.

SHANE

"*P*ick up," I muttered, pacing back and forth just outside the door to the brewery, "pick up, pick up, pick up."

Marcus tore out of the parking lot before I could reach him after it took me too long to recover from the shock of him running in the first place.

There was only one person I could think of who he might respond to in a moment when he wanted to escape the world.

Once upon a time, it would have been me.

Shoving aside the pain that came with acknowledging how far away we were from that place, where I was his lifeline to humanity in his moments of highest stress, I googled The Bake Place.

A sleek website with contact information and announcements about all kinds of new happenings for Ceecee and her bakery popped up.

I found the way to call in an order, and held my breath as I pushed the button.

"Cupcake Queen, this is Tyler. How can I make your day sweeter?"

Really? That was the opening for her special deliveries?

"Ceecee, I need to speak with Ceecee," I said, clutching my phone tighter. This was taking too damn long.

"I'm sorry, but Ceecee is busy in the kitchen at the moment. I can take your order."

"No. I need Ceecee. This is an emergency with her best friend, Marcus. Please, tell her Shane is calling. She'll take the call. Just, please." I spoke so fast my words ran together, but she had to answer the phone. I needed to make sure he was okay.

"Please hold," Tyler said, his voice sounding both suspicious and irritated, like he thought this was all a waste of time.

The sound of some soft music came over the line, and I wanted to throw my phone. The worst thing in the world when in a hurry: soft music that no one ever wants to listen to. It always made me feel like I was being patronized to like a child throwing a temper tantrum.

Finally, the music died, and Ceecee's frantic breaths filled the line.

"Shane? What did you do to Marcus? Is he okay?" she asked, voice a punishment.

"I didn't do anything, and I don't know if he's okay. I need you to check on him." I ran my hand through my hair, gripping onto it, and pulling as my pacing increased in speed.

"What? Why? He's at work. You had to have done something. I swear to God, Shane."

"No. He asked if I really left him a letter, and I said I did. I told him where I left it, and asked if he got it or not. Then he ran away. He sped out of the parking lot like he was on fire. Please, Ceecee. He's upset, and isn't answering his phone, and I don't know where he went, and he needs to be okay."

"You left him a letter?" she asked, and I yelled out a groaning scream noise.

"Of course, I did. But did you hear me? He's gone. I don't know where. Help me, Ceecee. He has to be okay. Please."

"I'm going to make sure he's okay, but not for you. You left him."

How did this get so screwed up? She hated me because I hurt her best friend, and that was fine. But how was she not getting that he was the important one here, right now? Not what happened back then.

"Damn it, I had to. Do you think I wanted to? I never wanted to leave him. Please. I'm begging. Help him."

"Just so you can hurt him all over again? He should have left that job and left you."

"Fine. I'm a terrible person, and I know I never deserved him. But you can yell at me later. Please. Find him. Make sure he's okay."

"You're right. You never deserved him, and I can't believe he still—I'll make sure he's okay. Just like I did last time. And now, you get to wait in the dark. Because I'm not going to tell you a thing. And if he never comes back to work for you, all the better."

She hung up.

That was it.

One minute I had Marcus right in front of me every day he was at work, and now…Because I opened my mouth and talked about the past, because I screwed up everything back then, I might not even have that after she spoke to him.

I looked at my phone, and hit the text icon. Marcus' number was right under Ceecee's.

Maybe you never want to hear from me again, and maybe that letter is long gone with the book to some secondhand store or the dump, but I remember every word.

Was I really going to do this? What else did I have to lose?

There was only one way to know if any of it mattered, if anything I did now would have any chance of making it okay, and if there was any hope left of him forgiving me.

I still couldn't take the risk of thinking we could be an us again, not really, but I didn't want him to leave and never come back…I needed him to come back. I needed to see him again.

Even if it meant watching as he went on with his life, found someone new, got married, and lived happily ever after. Knowing it was happening to him, seeing him happy, was worth losing him.

But this way?

Him running and me never knowing, never trusting what I managed to hear through mutters and rumors?

No. I couldn't handle it. Not after we finally had a chance to see each other again. Not after I finally had the chance to see him shine again.

Here it is:

Marcus, I love you. Before I write anything else, I need you to know that. I need you to feel that in your soul because I never want you to question the truth of the years we've spent together.

You will always be sunshine to me. No matter where I go, or what I do, seeing the sun will remind me of you.

When the light of it warms me, it will be you I feel.

That's what I'm taking with me, and I am sorrier than I can ever express that I can't leave you with more than these measly words.

But here they are anyway.

I love you. I will always love you. I have always loved you.

What I have to do now will not change that. And believe me I don't want to do it.

Something has happened. It doesn't matter what. But I need to take care of it. And no, you can't come with me.

You have a life here. You have a future here. One where you're going to do amazing things and shine like you were destined to.

I'm sorry. I can't take you from that.

This is on me. I understand if you hate me, if you never forgive me for this. But I don't know what else to do, how else to handle this.

All of this to say, I found out last night when I got home, and I had to choose. Right then.

My choice wasn't much of one.

The only thing I could think to do was this.

I'm leaving right now.

By the time you get done with classes today, I will be gone.

No one knows exactly where I'm going, except out of state. It has to be that way. Maybe one day I'll tell some people, those I keep in contact with.

It isn't because I want to keep this from you, but because I know if you find out, you'll insist on coming with me.

And I can't do that to you.

No matter how hard this is right now, I have to believe that it will be better for you in the future.

My one day is forever changed. I have no idea what it will look like now, or if it will even be much of a future at all whenever I finish what I need to. It may take a month or ten years. No one knows. Including me. But your one day can be as bright as you are.

Please, shine. I'll be watching for your light from where I need to go.

I will always love you, Sunny. Forever.

— Shane

Leaning back, tears running down my face, my phone blurred in front of me. I hit send on the last text, the last line of the letter I left him that broke me to write the first time.

Writing it out for him now was worse.

Something inside me tore open, the same wound as last time, but wider, deeper, and bleeding more freely.

Back then I thought I was doing the right thing for him no matter how bad it hurt.

Now...now I didn't know anything except I needed him. I couldn't lose the light in my life again. There was already too much darkness in the world.

MARCUS

Nothing about this new reality made any sense.

One day, I knew the way my world was, who the people in it were, their roles, whether I could trust them, all of it.

But now, I wasn't sure of anything.

"Marcus," Ceecee said, dropping to her knees in front of me, one of my shirts draped along her shoulders, hanging from the bar in my closet above her head.

"Shane," I said, holding out the paper to her, his words—hidden from me for years in a book in a tote in my closet—were smeared now, dotted with tears I cried for all the time I didn't know.

Ceecee took the paper from me, her eyes tight, and her mouth turned down in a frown.

"Read it," I said, not sure what to make of any of this, and needing someone else to tell me what to do.

My mind was too full of questions about the things I spent years telling myself. I couldn't think anymore, let alone make a decision.

She kept looking at me until I put a shaking hand to my mouth, and gestured with my head for her to look at the paper.

Finally, she looked down with a sigh, and began to read.

A chime went off in my pocket.

I should just leave it, ignore it like I did before, but watching Ceecee's face as emotions flickered across it was too much.

Pulling it out of my pocket, I saw Shane had called more than once, Ceecee called, and he sent multiple text messages.

Why I hit the button to read his texts, I didn't know. But even as my hands shook and the words swam in uneven waves in front of me, I opened the message and devoured them.

The same ones as in the letter.

But there was more after them, more he wanted to tell me, and I wasn't sure if I was ready.

I lowered my phone, and looked into Ceecee's eyes.

She was done reading, but I had no clue what she thought about any of it.

For the first time I could remember, her face was totally blank, and gave me no hint at what I should do.

"Ceecee, tell me," I said, begged really.

"Marcus." A little shake of her head and widening of her eyes was all I got from her. I didn't know anything more from that than her silence before.

"He gave me a letter. He…didn't leave me with no word. But it didn't explain what happened, and now…he sent me texts." I shoved the phone at her.

She blocked the phone with the paper in her hand, and her head shake turned almost violent as she grimaced.

"I can't read that. It's too…Marcus," she said, begging me right back.

"Please, Ceecee. I don't know what to do about any of this. Do I accept his word? Do I take him back? How am I supposed to pretend nothing happened, nothing was shattered when he left? What do I do? I can't read this. I don't know what to do right now."

"It's okay, Marcus. Shhh." She grabbed me, wrapped me up in her arms, and rubbed my back in soothing strokes.

"You don't have to do anything right now. Take your time. You're okay. I'm right here."

She kept talking to me, kept repeating that I had time, that I was okay.

But as much as I wanted it to be true, none of it was. I knew that.

Even as my best friend—the one who got me through it all last time—said the some of the same things, tried to reassure me, I didn't know how to accept her words.

I shook and cried, and begged her to tell me what to do.

Ceecee just kept repeating the same things, but her voice was just as full of pleading as mine was.

Finally, I was spent, and we were still on the floor of my closet with the tote full of the past open next to us, and a key to a possible future in my hand again.

"You don't have to read his messages right now. You can take your time," she said, her voice low and hoarse after speaking to me for so long.

My phone chimed again, and I dropped it.

It sat on the carpet next to us, as dangerous as a bomb, and, at the same time, a possible salvation.

"Can you just call him and tell him I need time?" I asked, my voice even weaker and more ragged than hers.

"No, but Theresa will do it," she said, taking her own phone out and giving me a wavering smile. "I need to let her know how you are anyway."

"Tell her I'm a mess?" My suggestion made her squeeze my hand tight, but her smile grew stronger.

She placed the call and held the phone out between us, the speaker on.

"Cee?" Theresa asked after a single ring as if her own phone was waiting in her hand for us to call.

"Marcus is going to be okay," Ceecee said, and I bit my lip wondering what they all thought I was going to do.

"Thank heavens," Theresa said, her voice markedly relieved. "Hang on, I'm telling the group."

"Everyone knows about this?" I asked.

"Because we all love you," Theresa said, her voice sounding as if she was offering me use of her heavy digging equipment again.

"How embarrassed should I be about this?" I asked, equal parts wanting to hide under my bed from all my friends without ever showing my face again, and intensely grateful for them all.

"You don't have to be embarrassed, Marcus," Theresa said. "We've all been through things, and we'll all go through more. It's just your turn."

"I'm not coming home tonight, Tee," Ceecee said, "I'll stay here with him, and call you in the morning."

"Um…" Theresa said.

"What, um? Should I be worried?" I asked, leaning toward the phone as if that would matter to what she was going to say next.

"Deacon and the others all want to bring food to Marcus. Are you up for that?" Theresa asked.

"Bunch of foodies," I muttered, shaking my head and not able to help the way the corners of my mouth turned up.

"Are you?" Ceecee asked, squeezing my hand again.

"Yeah. As long as none of them expect much from me tonight. Why not?" Maybe one of them would read his texts for me.

"Good. We'll be there soon. Gotta go."

"Wait, Theresa!" I still needed to ask her to call Shane, but she had already hung up.

I looked at Ceecee, wondering what she would think of her

girlfriend's sudden sign-off, but she was smiling fondly at the screen as she tucked her phone away.

"Maybe we can call her back and—" I was cut off from finishing what I was going to say by my doorbell ringing.

"No way," I yelled, my hoarse voice turning into a croak.

"Come on," Ceecee said, getting up and grabbing my hand to pull me to my feet. "I bet she was in her truck in the parking lot the whole time we were on the phone."

"But why?" I asked, not understanding at all how she was just chilling in the parking lot of my building with no way of knowing if we would even call. What was her plan?

"Tee is protective. If she saw Shane out there while we were in here, and she didn't know for a fact he was wanted, she would have run interference and checked with us before she let him pass."

"You knew about this?"

"No. But I know her." Ceecee reached out and pulled open my front door.

With a quick kiss on Ceecee's lips, Theresa came in and wrapped me in a hug, too.

"Look at me," Theresa said, leaning back and staring into my eyes, her arms still around me, strong on my back, "do we need concrete?"

"Stop," I said, bending and resting my head on her shoulder. "No matter what happens, no one is allowed to hurt him."

"Oh, no. He's still got it bad," Theresa said above me to Ceecee, but there was a smile in her voice.

"You have no idea how bad," I said. The tears came again, not as wrung out as I thought, and the words were garbled.

"Come on," Ceecee said, helping Theresa led me to the couch. "He needs to read the texts that—"

As she spoke my phone chimed again in my hand and I jumped, almost dropping it.

"That Shane is still sending," Ceecee finished.

"We aren't reading them because..." Theresa let the half question hang in the air as I curled up on the couch, Ceecee on one side of me and Theresa on the other, creating a buffer for me from the world.

"Because I can't," I said, not even knowing fully why. "What if they really are a goodbye? That all this was too much? He left once, and his letter didn't explain why. Maybe he's going to leave again. Maybe he wants me to be the one to do it this time."

"Give me the phone," Theresa said, holding out her hand.

"No, Tee," Ceecee said, "this is between them. He needs to read them."

Theresa sighed, "Fine, but at some point tonight, those texts are getting read."

"And that's why I wanted you to call him," I said.

"Wait, me?" Theresa shook her head, already trying to refuse.

I grabbed both her hands, shoving the phone into one of hers in the process.

"Yes, you. You're not afraid to tell someone to shut up and listen and wait. I can't tell him. I'm not ready, and I need time. But you can."

"But I might screw it up," Theresa said, her voice soft and more scared than I had ever heard her. "That's a lot of pressure."

"No. No pressure," I said, trying to beg her without begging too much and making it obvious exactly how important this was to me.

"Marcus, let's just wait a little longer," Ceecee said, and we all dropped the subject.

While they talked about the others bringing food, I stayed curled in a ball, the phone burning in my hand, screaming at me to look at it, to call him.

But Theresa was right. There was a lot riding on what happened right now.

And I still had no idea what I wanted to do.

"What is going on here?" Van asked, whirling into my office as if she were about to light into me like she did her kids when they got out of hand.

"I don't know," I said, my head in my hands, and my focus going back and forth between her and the phone sitting on my desk in front of me, still silent.

"People said Marcus ran out crying, and you ran out after him. Andrew…" She planted her hands on her hips, and leveled her big mama gaze at me, the one that I found strangely terrifying even though my own mother never gave me that look while she was alive.

"He didn't know, Van," I said, telling her everything, catching her up to the utter disaster I landed myself in this time.

"You still haven't told him about your mom?" she asked. Her arms dropped to her sides, and she slid into one of the chairs on the other side of my desk as if that fact made it hard for her to stand.

"It feels like an excuse." I didn't know how to explain why I didn't want to tell him the full reason I left.

"She needed you. It was hard for you. That isn't an excuse. That's the truth, and he deserves the truth."

Van was right, but it was more than hard. Even now, talking about it at all was enough to make me want to hide away in her little house, and never go outside again.

"And how do I explain why I didn't come back right away when I had the chance?" That was the biggest problem. I could have come back over two years ago, the same time we started the brewery.

Technically, I could have come back.

But I assumed he had moved on. I thought there was no chance that the brightest light I ever had in my life wouldn't have found someone that appreciated his shine. And I couldn't mess that up for him.

"You keep making decisions for him, Shane. You keep assuming things about him, his life, and what he wants."

"I want him to be happy. I want to make his life easier. I am not easier."

"No. You're an idiot. You're difficult. But that isn't why."

"Then what's the reason, oh wise one?" I threw my hands in the air, more than done with her cryptic ways of trying to tell me I was wrong.

"Because you keep treating him like the teenager he was when you met. You keep treating him like the fragile flower he was when his parents pushed him out, when they told him he was dead to them. But any guy who survived that, and then managed to keep going after you left him for reasons he still doesn't know, isn't fragile."

"Marcus is amazing just as he is. I just don't want to hurt him." I shoved up from the desk, and leaned toward her, yelling now, not caring if people could hear us through the door.

"You just want to protect him to the point that you're the one hurting him." She shoved up from the desk, too, and yelled right back at me.

"I do not." I ran my hands over my face, not wanting to listen to this right now. This wasn't time to think about myself. This was time to focus on Marcus.

"No matter how many times you say it, and no matter how much you may convince yourself, I know the truth." She pointed a finger at me, and it felt like an accusation.

"Stop. You're really yelling at me now? He might never speak to me again." I put my hands over my eyes, and flopped back into my chair, shaking my head, not wanting to hear any more.

"And whose fault would that be? He needs to know the truth, and you need to trust him with it." There was that finger again, pointing at me as her words stabbed me.

"Of course, I trust him." I gripped the armrests of my chair, forcing myself to stay seated this time. Somehow, I had to avoid making this even worse.

"If you really trusted him, you would tell him everything. You not trusting him to make his own damn decisions, like a grown man, is what caused all this in the first place. Then, you didn't trust him to accept you when you had the first chance to come back. Now, you still won't trust him with the whole story. For all he knows, you left him to go start a brewery. Think, Andrew."

Finally, she shook her head, and slumped into her own chair, staring across the desk at me.

She let her words hang in the air, waiting for me to hear them. Not just listen to her yelling, but actually hear them.

They ran through my head, and I tried to look past all the fears and the years of trying to tell myself that what I did was okay.

But none of my old excuses mattered anymore. Now, they all sank beneath the weight of her accusations. And further beneath her revelation about me not trusting him.

"Was that what I did? Did I make it seem like I didn't trust him to make his own decisions?" I finally asked, my voice a weak shudder of what it had been.

"Maybe he didn't see it that way, but I always did. You took his choices away from him, Andrew. You need to apologize for that, no matter the reason you did it."

Dropping my face into my hands, I leaned on my desk again.

Yes, I needed to apologize for what I did, for the specifics. And I needed to trust him with the truth, no matter how scared I was about his reaction.

I picked up my phone, my hand shaking, and pulled up the string of texts I sent him. All the ways I had asked how he was. And all the ways I had begged him to talk to me.

None of them told him the story, the truth.

Swallowing, I looked up at Van again, to someone who would be here for me if it wasn't enough for him to forgive me.

Finally, one word at a time, I told him the story.

My mother had Alzheimers.

She didn't tell me. She wouldn't let anyone tell me for quite a while, and relied on Zeda, Van, other friends, caretakers.

Until she couldn't anymore.

In the middle of all of that. Cancer struck.

The call I got was to tell me she had bone cancer, and had fallen and broken her hip. That's how they found the cancer.

They told me she had limited time, but they didn't know how limited. A month. Years. They weren't sure. But she needed me. And after so many years of only seeing her once in a while, I had to go.

So, I left.

I can't explain to you how sorry I am that I didn't tell you what was going on, or why I was leaving.

At the time I told myself that none of the time I was about to spend taking care of her, none of the pain I was about see her go through, or go through myself, should be put on you.

But now I wonder if it just was a really messed up way of trying to protect you when I should have trusted you.

I'm sorry. I'm sorry for not telling you what was going on.

And I'm sorry that I was so scared of you rejecting me that I didn't come back as soon as she was out of pain, and I was free to come home.

But most of all, I'm sorry that it took me this long after I saw you again to come clean.

Marcus, I know you may not forgive me for taking your choice in the matter from you over and over again.

I...will have to accept if you don't forgive me. Because I'm not taking your choice from you this time.

No matter what you decide, please know, it's always been you.

When we were together, it was you. I loved you.

When I left, it was you. I loved you then, too.

When I was caring for my dying mother, and crying myself to sleep, it was still you. I loved you, even when I tried to let you go.

When she passed, and Van and I started the brewery as some strange way to heal and keep moving, it was you. I named this place after the one I still loved. After the last name that I wanted to join with mine.

When you walked in the door, and surprised me, it was you.

And even watching you run out today, it's still you. It has always been you.

I looked up at Van, and wiped the tears dripping down my chin.

She gave me a soft smile and nodded.

"He might never come back, and never want to talk to me again," I said, my voice a strangled sound as if I was choking on the possibility already.

"Or," she said, leaning across the desk, and folding her

fingers around mine, "when he comes back this time, he'll be doing it knowing and accepting everything."

Nodding, I turned my hand, and squeezed hers back. I hoped she was right. If she was, this was a new beginning, not an end.

It seemed like it took forever and no time at all for my loud gaggle of friends to arrive, all of them carrying something, and letting themselves in after Ceecee yelled at them to quit knocking.

With a pizza box in hand, Katie stopped right in front of me, and cocked her head, a sympathetic smile on her face even as she looked as tired as I felt in the uniform of sweats and messy hair that I recognized from my own college days.

"You look like lesbian book ends of a very sad, gay story," Katie said.

"Katie," Olivia yelled, her mouth falling open.

Deacon just shut his eyes and sighed.

But I laughed. I couldn't help it.

For some reason, being a very sad, gay story with my own personal lesbian book ends was the funniest thing I had ever heard.

"Come here," I said, standing up and opening my arms.

She made a happy squeal noise, put the pizza box down on my coffee table, and wrapped her arms around me.

"Thank you for making me laugh," I said.

"You're welcome," she said, pulling back from me, and landing a smack of a kiss on my cheek. "Now, your Shane is really hot. So, what did he do?"

"Katie," Campbell yelled this time from where he and Olivia were laying out tons of food on my bar counter that looked over the kitchen.

In answer, Katie just stuck her tongue out at him.

"She's fine," I said, rubbing a hand over my face as Deacon grabbed me and swung me off my feet in a hug.

"You sure you don't want all the guys to come over and be your boyfriends again?" he asked.

"More than sure. That just left everyone confused. But thank you." I patted his arm as he set me back down, that bright smile on his face.

"Eat something, Marcus," Olivia said, coming from the vast array of food to give me a hug, too, plus a pouty and concern-filled smile.

"Ordering you around and feeding you is her way of saying she loves you," Campbell said, wrapping us both up in a hug.

"I appreciate it. Truly," I said, which was the truth, but I still wasn't sure if I would be able to eat anything, even if it was all delicious food from Joe's.

"Now, tell me," Katie said, grabbing my arm and tugging me toward my spot between Ceecee and Theresa on the couch.

After a deep breath and a glance at Ceecee and Theresa, I caught them all up.

By the time I was done, Olivia was trying not to cry, and flapping her hands at her face to get her eyes to stop welling up. Campbell rubbed her back. Deacon just sat with wide eyes, staring at the floor, and everyone was camped out all over my living room.

Including Katie, who was perched on the coffee table next to the open box of pizza she carried in, chewing on a bite of her second slice, her face lit up like she was watching a bad soap opera.

"Hand me the phone," she said, swallowing her bite of pizza and holding out her hand.

"No. Katie, I don't think that's a good idea," Ceecee said, sitting up straighter.

"Yes," Katie said, setting a hard gaze on Ceecee. "If no one else will call him and tell him Marcus is fine and just needs time, then let me."

I held my phone out to her.

Ceecee and Theresa both looked like I was making a terrible mistake, but Katie grinned and set her pizza slice down in the lid of the box next to her.

She held the phone out to me, so I opened it and pushed the button. She wiggled as she put it on speaker, and I sunk into the couch, rethinking every decision I ever made.

"Marcus?" Shane's voice, a tremulous exhalation more than a statement or a question, came through the speaker. I squeezed my eyes shut, pressing the back of my hand against my mouth so I didn't say anything. Or worse. Sob.

"This is Marcus' friend, Katie," she said. Her voice sounded far too excited for the circumstances, and I latched onto Ceecee's hand with my free one.

"Is he okay?" Shane asked, and something thudded on his end of the phone.

"He's fine. We're with him now. But you screwed up, dude. So, he's going to take some time, you're going to stop texting and calling, and give him the time he needs."

All I heard were his heavy, shuddering breaths, and I bent my head, trying to block out the image of him crying.

"Okay. I…understand. Has he…Did he read my texts?"

"No. But he will. He just needs to process. That letter is new to him, you know?"

"Yeah…I…He…Oh, god, I can't even talk."

"Well, you should see Marcus."

At that, my eyes popped open, and I glared at Katie. What was she doing?

"Please. Please tell me he's okay."

She grinned.

"Can I ask you something in return?"

"Yes, of course. Anything he needs."

"Do you love him?"

He laughed, but I knew that laugh, and it made my heart beat harder in my chest.

"More than I can say. He's alright? Really? I didn't...I don't want to mess things up for him all over again."

"This is hard, but our Marcus is strong. He will be okay. And, in the meantime, he's got all of us. He'll be alright. Just give him time, Shane."

"Thank you. Thank you."

"Gotta go now. Bye, Shane." Katie hit the button on my phone and smiled at me, leaning forward to pat me on the knee. "Did that help?"

I couldn't speak, but I leaned forward and hugged her as she giggled.

"You all should trust me a lot more," Katie said, shaking her head as we pulled apart. "Now I'm going to read these texts."

"Katie," Campbell and Olivia said at the same time as Deacon groaned and swiped the phone from her hand.

"Hey. Deek," Katie yelled, trying to snatch it back from him.

"Those are private."

"For Marcus only."

"We shouldn't touch those."

"Leave those alone."

Everyone chimed in with something to say while I just took my phone out of Deacon's hand, ending the argument before it really got started.

I looked down at the phone in my hand, and then around at my friends.

"Actually," I said, "I'm going to read them."

They all stopped, frozen in place as if they weren't sure if I was telling them the truth.

"Marcus, are you sure?" Ceecee asked. "You don't have to rush."

"Yeah," I said, nodding and looking at the phone in my hand before I slipped it into my pocket. "I'm going to look at them. I need to. But first, I want a piece of pizza."

SHANE

"Go home, Andrew," Zeda said, leaning her head into my doorway.

"You should have left hours ago. Why are you telling me that?" I asked the ceiling, leaning back in my chair and stuck in the same place I had been for so long I could barely feel my feet.

"Because, as part of the party, I had a lot of extra work to do, but I know you need to sleep. What's wrong with you now? Did Marcus tell you he never wants to see you again?"

I didn't entirely think through all the additional work that our plan created for Zeda. I factored it into the additional restaurants and distributions we were doing, but not the competition.

Maybe I was a bad friend as well as a bad ex-boyfriend.

"No. A friend of his said he needed time. Which…is good I think." I tilted my head so I could look at her better. "I'm sorry so much has landed on your plate, Z."

"We both know I'm only here because I like what I do, so don't worry about it."

I smiled at her before my face fell back into the blank mask that felt like it had taken up semi-permanent residence there. I looked at the ceiling again.

"So…" she said, sitting in one of my chairs.

"So, what, Z?"

One of the best things about Zeda was that I almost never had to wonder what she thought because she would come right out and say it. But every now and then that meant she assumed I knew what she was getting at when I didn't. Now was one of those times. And I lacked the ability to expend enough mental energy to try and puzzle it out.

"Marcus knows now."

"Yep."

"And what are you going to do to get him back?" she asked with all the inflection of someone asking about the bus routes, not one of the most important things to happen in my life, whether I would have him in it or not.

"What, exactly, do you think I should be doing to get him back?" I sat up then. My back, angry from being in the same position for far too long, screamed at me as I did. But that ache was easy to forget. The one that sprung up in my heart at what I could offer Marcus was harder to ignore.

"I'm not sure I'm any good at the whole love thing." Zeda wrinkled her nose as if the entire prospect of being in love with someone was slightly distasteful, like it was her least favorite flavor of jam, and that's all that was left to put on her toast.

"Maybe not, but you wouldn't have brought it up if you didn't have something to say to me about it."

She grinned at me because we both knew that was true.

Zeda leaned forward to rest her elbows on the desk between us, and looked off to the side, thinking through whatever she was going to tell me.

It should have set my nerves further on edge. Especially after they spent the day being frayed beyond their usual breaking point by everything going on with Marcus. But Zeda was as calming a presence as she always was when I was taking care of my mother.

There were times when Zeda made it harder for me to keep my cool about something. But when the world was more trying than I thought I could manage, Zeda had an ability to remain so unflappable that it lent me some of her strength. That was only a problem when I wanted someone to be upset about something with me. She was not the kind of friend to turn to in those moments.

Now, though…Now she was a welcome calm to this storm I felt bearing down on me.

"Do you remember when your mom first passed away, and you were planning her service?" Zeda finally asked, and all the good feeling about her being in here with me fled down the hall to hide in the experiment room waiting to make a batch sour.

"Yes," I said when her silence proved she was waiting for an answer even if I didn't want to give her one.

I had far too many memories stored from that time.

"And do you remember what you told me about Marcus when I asked if you were going to contact him and tell him about it?" She cocked her head to the side and stared at me.

"Of course, I do." I swallowed, the words like stones in my mouth.

"Well, do you still think he deserves something more than a, 'Hey, here I am with a lot more emotional baggage,' or what?" she asked it as if she was just curious, with none of the accusation that I turned the words into.

Because, for me, they were an accusation. I spent so long saying that, making that a reason not to reach out and risk him turning me away. But just because it was an excuse, it didn't mean it wasn't true.

Leaning forward, I stretched out my back at the same time I rubbed the heels of my hands into my tired eyes.

"Do you have any suggestions for grand, romantic gestures I

could give to the guy I left too long ago, and just now thought possible to have back again? Because I have to be honest, Z. I have been staring at the ceiling waiting for the plan to appear for a while, and I'm drawing a blank."

She didn't say anything, so I looked up at her. She had her head to the side, her gaze unfocused on the wall.

"Would he be the kind of the person who wouldn't mind something public, or would he prefer something quiet and private?"

"Are you actually thinking about helping me come up with something good? Because I don't think the flowers and dinner route will be good enough for this." Rubbing my fingers along my cheeks, I tried to think through the million ideas I came up with and then discarded. Maybe going through them again in my head would lead me to something I could turn into a real possibility.

"Not that I'm thinking about coming up with something right for you two. I don't know your relationship, or either of you well enough to find the perfect thing." She shook her head, and I furrowed my brow.

More than almost anyone else in my life, Zeda knew about our relationship from my end.

"How can you say you don't know well enough? I've told you a lot about Marcus and I."

"You have. He hasn't." She waved a hand as if I said something silly that didn't warrant a thoughtful response. "Besides, no one really understands a relationship from the outside, least of all one like yours."

"What do you mean, 'one like ours?'" I held my breath, hoping she didn't mean a broken one.

"A relationship so deep in your souls neither of you could move on from it. Most people would have by now. Instead, you two spent years knowing that what you had was so rare, it would be foolish to try and find it again. And before you argue with that, I do know enough about him to know that's true."

I could barely breathe now—not because I saw us as broken or because her words hurt, but because I saw the ways in which we were still whole.

"Maybe there are a couple things I could do for him," I said, my voice thin.

Biting my lip on a smile that wanted to be sprinkled with the tears I fought to keep at bay, I looked at Zeda in silent thanks.

She just grinned at me, probably knowing full well what she managed to do with a few words.

"You know," I said, getting my voice back under control, "Van's party might be a great opportunity." I finally stood, my legs and back crying out in protest at the movement that seemed unnatural from so long not put to use.

Zeda stood up, too, and patted me on the shoulder.

"I was thinking the same thing."

MARCUS

"Are you sure you're ready for this?" Ceecee asked for the thousandth time.

"Yeah. And when I'm done, I'll come out and give you all the updates," I smiled at a still-perturbed Katie, and turned toward my room. She really wanted to be the one reading them.

Not shutting the door all the way, leaving a crack so they could hear me wail if it went badly, just as we planned, I went to my bed and sat down.

Taking a bomb to bed with me was what it felt like to hold the phone in my hand and open the texts.

Scrolling through the first frantic attempts to check on me and the whole of the letter he repeated, I found the newer messages.

I really wanted to do this in person. Well, that's not entirely true. Part of me hoped we would never need to have this conversation, that you would magically just know all of this. But that's because when it comes to you, I'm a coward.

You mean so much to me that it makes me weak and stupid and afraid.

But, here goes.

Shane told me the real reason he left, and my heart broke all over again. This time, though, it broke for him, not because of him.

Of all the reasons I entertained over the years, I never got close to the real one.

And, for as much as he was sorry and he wished he did it differently, I understood.

He was there for me when I lost my parents. I was there for him when his dad passed. And I wished I could have been there for him to help with his mom. At the same time, I understood why a college kid made the decision he did.

What hurt wasn't that he put me through so much by leaving, or that he took my choice away from me.

The first pain was like an old break that ached when it rained. I knew it as well as my own face, and it wasn't something that could tear me open in the same way.

For the new information, the new pain of my choice in the matter being taken from me, it was lessened by the knowledge that it was done out of a foolish desire to spare me.

As if, in the sparing, I had to lose a finger. Small in comparison, but it still left me sore and changed.

Especially because he was changed by it. He knew it was wrong of him. And I didn't think he would do it again. I wasn't planning on letting him.

Surprising myself, there were few tears that fell with all of his messages.

Maybe I really had run out.

But the ones that did, fell from happiness. Because my Shane, the love of my life, who never left the part of my heart and soul that was stamped all over with his name, still loved me. Had always loved me.

Part of me, the contrary and petty part, wondered if there was anything Shane could have done to make me love him less.

It didn't matter, really.

There were so many ugly and terrible reasons I dreamt up in the dark days after he left, even if I tried to throw them aside, pretend that I never thought them, and refused to speak them out loud, they had crossed my mind.

And even then, when those cruel possible reasons for him leaving entered my mind and tortured me in the night when I couldn't pack my days full of distractions, I still loved him.

So, when his reason for leaving me turned out to be a wayward yet noble act of someone so in love that he tried to save the person in his heart by cutting out his own, it only made me love him more. Even if it hurt.

"Fool," I muttered to my phone, and started to type out a message back to him.

But I paused. A wild idea entered into my head, and I deleted everything I typed.

I didn't want to do this over text any more than he did. I wanted to do this in person.

Wiping my face and taking a deep breath, I held the phone against my chest as if I was able to hug his words closer to me, as if I was able to hug him to me even as he was further away from me than I wanted him to be.

Eventually, I remembered my friends were waiting for me in my living room, and probably getting worried about me in here.

Or they just thought Shane sent me that many texts to read.

Smiling to myself, I shoved off the bed and stretched, more than ready to begin to work on getting Shane back so I could hold him instead of the stupid electronic device in my arms.

Finally, pulling open my door, I found all my friends, whispering to each other, heads close together as if they were afraid to be too loud and upset me while I went through his messages.

They turned as one to look at me, and I grinned.

"A long time ago," I said into the silence, "my parents threw me out and disowned me because I'm gay. The best friend they thought was spending nights playing video games and hanging out was actually my boyfriend, and we were probably doing things they didn't approve of."

"Where are they now?" Theresa asked, her voice as hard as the heavy machinery she kept threatening Shane with, and made me think she wanted to use it on my parents.

"It doesn't matter." I shook my head. Truly, it didn't matter. Not anymore.

"Yes, it does. Tell us," Katie said, and she and Theresa shared a look that made me realize which friends of mine were the really dangerous ones.

"No. It did at one point. They broke my heart, and Shane helped me put the pieces back together. But I wanted to tell you all that they did me a favor."

They shared glances as if they didn't understand what I was talking about at all.

Everyone but Ceecee, who just gave me a loving smile.

"Because while I was reading and processing Shane's messages, I realized that my family now—the one waiting in my living room to help me deal with whatever was going to happen next—was better than the family I was born to."

I didn't have to say anything else. They all got up from their seats, some of them with wet eyes, and I got another round of hugs as I explained what Shane told me about his mother, and about him still loving me.

Ceecee pulled me by the hand back to the spot on the couch between her and Theresa.

Even though we were all a lot fuller after indulging in Olivia's version of love, we all went back to our spots in my living room, much lighter than the last time we all settled there.

"Well," Katie said, "now that we know you and your man are both still crazy about each other, why are you still here with us?"

"Katie," I said this time, shaking my head.

"Seriously," she said, grinning, "why don't you just go to him right now, and kiss him hard enough he forgets his own name? He's sexier than we are."

"Please," Deacon said, "speak for yourself."

We all laughed at that while Deacon beamed like a little kid, making sexy a word that made no sense for him.

I'm sure there were some football fans and people he knew who thought he was sexy, but he really was too pure for this world. I could only ever see him as cute.

Of course, that made sense. I could appreciate the beauty in each of my friends, they each had their own form of it, but the only person I had ever thought truly sexy, the only one I ever wanted to even kiss was Shane.

"Right now, as much as I want to do just that, Katie," I smiled at her wicked grin and the wiggle of her eyebrows, "I would rather do something, plan something that would be a big restart to our relationship. Not just a kiss."

"Just a kiss?" Olivia said, looking at Campbell in a way that made me think there was a story about a kiss somewhere in the way they got together that I really needed to hear one day.

"Sometimes, Marcus," Campbell said, but he was looking at Olivia and pulled her in tighter to him the look on his face mirroring hers, "a kiss can change your world."

"While they reminisce," Theresa said, smiling and shaking her head at them, "why do I think you have a plan, Marcus, and you're about to ask all of us to help you?"

That drew all their attention back to me, and I didn't even try to suppress the wide smile on my face.

"Because that's exactly what I'm about to say."

Exchanging glances that ranged from thrilled to mischievous, they all nodded. I knew they would help me in every way they could, because this family stood up for each other.

"First, though," I said, turning to look at Olivia and Campbell with a brow raised high, "I want to hear about this world-changing kiss."

"*D*o you have everything, Van?" I asked as she loaded another box of stuff into the trunk of her car.

"Yes. Finally," she smiled at me, and shut the trunk. "If everyone stops giving me things, then, yes, I've got it all."

"That's a pretty good reason to be overpacked." I grinned and put an arm over her shoulder. "Everyone here loves you, and we'll all miss you. But I'm going to miss you more than anyone else."

"I know, but we both knew this day was coming." She wrapped an arm around my waist and squeezed.

"Knowing a thing, expecting it even, and actually living it are different things."

"Speaking of," her grin formed a wicked and scheming edge, "are *you* ready for tonight?"

"No. Not at all." I laughed and shook my head, trying not show exactly how scared I was in case someone saw me, and thought I was freaking out that Van was leaving. That wouldn't exactly garner trust in the business after she was gone.

"What are you talking about? This is your chance. This is what you've wanted for years."

"Yeah," I muttered, unable to even put words to the way she wasn't helping me at all. Mentioning how long I waited for this chance and how little I expected it to actually be real only increased my anxiety. "He still hasn't committed to coming tonight."

"He hasn't told you. That doesn't mean he's not coming. I'm positive he's coming to the party." She smiled and there was a spring in her step that had been missing for a while.

"Van." I shook my head, not wanting to have this conversation. It made it all that much worse.

"Let's go see how Zeda is doing." She led me through the door, both of us unlinking our arms to make it inside and navigate the kitchen easier.

There was a lot riding on Zeda and her experiments. She had all the lists, and all the information. The crew had long since abandoned the lists we put up for them to write their information about their brews on.

Having this party in the middle of the week when the tasting room was normally closed meant that walking through the kitchen and behind the bar was like going through a maze of bodies.

"At least everyone else came to work today," I said once Van and I were at Zeda's door.

"You can't be mad that he's been avoiding you," she said, hands on her hips.

"I'm not. That wasn't a comment on Marcus."

She seemed to be okay with that as she opened the door, but it was the truth. I wasn't mad. I couldn't be. She was right. I was concerned it meant he wasn't coming back. Tonight, or ever.

No matter how much this place was my baby, and I thought of the contest we were kicking off tonight as his, that didn't mean he thought of it that way.

Why would he?

He knew now that I started this place instead of going back to him as soon as I could. Maybe he hated it and never wanted to see it again, let alone step inside and be part of saving it in its current form.

The only way I would know for sure would be if he came through the doors and told me, one way or another.

It would serve me right if he left me wondering forever.

Zoned out, lost in my own head over thoughts of Marcus and the party tonight, and my plans for seeing him again, I admitted the truth to myself. Even if Marcus didn't choose me, I didn't really believe he would ghost me.

Fear plagued me, made me second-guess everything because he was so important, and what happened at the party would be so important. But I had a hard time believing Marcus would ever make the same mistakes I did.

He was better than me.

"Stop it with that face," Zeda said, snapping me back to the room. She and Van were staring at me as if I missed something they said before.

"I'm sorry, what?" I asked.

"Your face. Stop it," Zeda said with a gesture up toward her own screwed up face and nose.

"This is my face. It doesn't change. What are you talking about?" I wasn't crying or grimacing or anything. She wasn't making any sense.

"No. That isn't your normal face," Zeda said, and Van just put a hand up to cover her mouth like she was trying to hide laughter or a grin.

Great, they were laughing at me.

"Come on," I said, not wanting to have an attack-on-Andrew session where they told me I was being ridiculous. Tonight really was that damn important, and I wasn't overreacting.

"You come on," Zeda said, sounding outright irritated. "You

walk in here, don't listen to what I'm saying, and stand around with that half-lovestruck, half-morose look in your face, and I don't like it."

"Well, excuse me." I threw my hands in the air. "I just wanted to come in here and see if..."

I swallowed, unable to finish my sentence.

Because now that I was in here, I didn't have the guts to actually ask.

"There it is," Zeda said, shaking her head.

"Stop, Z," I said, putting a hand up, palm out to her, begging her not to go on with what she was going to say. This was all too much for me, and even as I got my head around it one minute, the gravity of the situation fell on me the next.

No matter what they wanted from me right now, I was going to be a mess until I knew for sure that he showed up. Or that he didn't.

I was in here looking for clues as to what he would do, but there was no way to know for sure until I saw him, until I spoke with him. And no amount of pretending otherwise would make the intervening hours any easier to get through.

"Were you this pathetic last time you were with Marcus?" Zeda asked, and a snicker leaked out of Van's mouth as she pressed her lips together tightly. "No wonder you acted like a big baby and ran away."

"Don't you dare," I yelled, pointing at both of them.

"What?" Zeda yelled. "Tell you the truth? Expect you to act like this matters, and you're willing to fight for it?"

"Both of you know I would do anything for him. If I need to fight for a chance to get him back, then fine. That makes me the opposite of a baby."

Zeda smiled, and all the tension of her posture relaxed while a small laugh made it out of Van as she dropped her hand, revealing her wild smile.

"Good," Zeda said, "that's all I wanted to hear."

I looked back and forth between them as they both grinned at me and shared in a quiet moment of laughter.

"Excuse me," I yelled, "what was that?"

"We just needed to be sure you weren't going to wimp out, and do nothing when it came time to make your move," Zeda said, leaning back against one of the counters.

They were kidding. They had to be. None of this made any sense.

"How could you think I wouldn't do anything? Have you been paying any attention?"

"Yeah," Van said, still smiling like this was hilarious, "We have been paying attention to you second-guessing everything, and standing around working with him every day while you pine and whine and don't do anything to get him back."

"Great to know what you both actually think of me." My cousin and my best friend were traitors, and had no faith in me. Fantastic. I was thrilled.

"Andrew," Van said, her smile falling as she sighed, "what we actually think of you is that you deserve better than you've allowed yourself to believe."

"What? Then why are you both acting like I'm going to screw this up, and that I'm the world's biggest whiner?" They still weren't making any sense.

"Because, Boss," Zeda said, "you've spent years beating yourself up over what happened between you while you let the torch you carry for him burn you over and over again, thinking you deserve the pain. But you don't."

"I don't?" My voice was little more than a breath, but I was lucky anything came out of my throat.

These women who I loved, who were beside me as I forced myself to keep going the last few years, had stoked my anger to the point of yelling. And now they were telling me they did it out of love. I wasn't sure I would ever be able to make sense of any of this. But for some reason it made me want to cry, and hold them both close.

"No," Van said, "you deserve for him to forgive you, and for him to make you suffer for a few days like he has."

Zeda laughed at that, and I took a deep breath, deciding against the hug.

"But you also came clean to him," Van said, her voice softer now, "learned from this, and you deserve to have him give you another chance."

"Are you sure you don't want anyone to come with you tonight?" Theresa asked, pulling up in front of The Big O organic coffee shop.

"I appreciate you coming with me to get all this ready," I said, unbuckling my seatbelt, "but this is something I need to show up to on my own. Just knowing that you all will be there somewhere will be enough."

"Okay, but I want that coffee," she said, giving me a look as if she was checking that I remembered her order.

"Yes, Ma'am." I smiled and got out of her truck, "Just don't let me wait on this curb too long."

"Never," she said, as I shut the door.

Theresa pulled away, her truck too big to hang out in the little parking lot for however long this was going to take.

I walked across the lot toward the green exterior of my favorite coffee shop, The Big O, a great coffee place with open mic nights and rotating art on the walls from local artists of all kinds.

For right now, the coffee I was picking up for myself and

Theresa was just a bonus. The art was the reason for my visit today.

Once inside, I took a minute to look around at the art for this week. Everything reminded me of drizzly days in Seattle in the Spring. It was beautiful, soft, and ethereal, as if they were all painted by someone who fell in love with the rain.

"Marcus," Gray yelled from behind the counter, his voice loud over the low hum of the music, and yet the few people at the tables in the room didn't even twitch at the sound.

"Hey, is your wife here?" I asked with a wave. Gray and his wife were the biggest reason why I loved the vibe of this place. They were welcoming and outgoing and made me feel like I was visiting them at their house every time I came in, no matter how many others in here were strangers to me.

"Oh, I see how you are. Ignore me, and just ask for my beautiful wife. Although, I didn't think she was your type, Marcus."

Gray's grin was wicked, and I couldn't help laughing.

"She's not, but then again, neither are you."

He put a hand to his chest and stumbled back against the counter behind him, which only made me laugh louder as I made my way to him.

Not that Gray wasn't cute with his long black hair and his dark eyes. He just wasn't Shane. And he wasn't single.

"I know, I know," Gray said, shaking his head and smiling, "your type is the mysterious love you won't give me details about. But I'll go get Benni for you."

With a light slap on my hand across the counter that was his usual way of showing affection, he went into the back for just a second, his wife, Benni, following after him on his way back out.

"Marcus," she said, her smile soft and motherly even if she was my age.

"Hi. Did it come?" I asked.

"Yes," she said, nodding to her husband who stepped up to

the counter ready to take my order, "I'll get it. You get a coffee. And maybe when you're full of warmth, you'll explain to me what this is for?"

She winked and walked to the door to the office on the other side of the space behind the main counter.

"Do you want a drink?" Gray asked, bringing me back to Theresa's request.

"Two, actually," I said.

"Oh, two? Who are we getting a coffee for, then?" he asked. "Is it the unnamed love?"

"No. This is a girl, Theresa, Ceecee's girlfriend." I shook my head, but I couldn't suppress my smile at his constantly wanting me to have someone in my life beyond the story that I had told him of the man I loved.

"Well, she should have come in. I would love to meet Ceecee's girlfriend."

"Sorry, I'll bring her in another time."

He took my order, and went about the process of getting our coffees with the practiced ease of someone who knew every inch of the space they worked in. It reminded me of Ceecee when she was in her bakery.

"If you're here now, does that mean you won't be coming to open mic tonight?" he asked over his shoulder.

Leaning on the counter, I tried to remember the last time I was able to come to one of my favorite middle-of-the-week events in the city.

"Unfortunately, I won't make it tonight. But I don't usually work on Wednesdays anymore at this new job, so hopefully soon."

"That would be great. The regulars miss your cheering." He winked at me over his shoulder as he set aside one cup and went to work on the other.

I loved open mics, but I never performed. I just liked to

watch everyone else get up there, and create something out of thin air.

"Here it is," Benni said, coming out of the back, carrying a huge, thin bag with rope handles.

"Did you look at it?" I asked, running over to her and taking the handle, barely able to stop myself from ripping open the packaging and getting a peek.

"No," Benni said.

"She wanted to," Gray added, and she grinned at him, shaking her head.

"But Lilliana showed me her design mockup," Benni said. "Is it really going to be on t-shirts? Because I would love to get one."

"That would be great. I hope everyone likes it as much as you do." I smiled, and paid for the coffees. "Thank you both, and I'll see you later. I have to go to this thing, and there's still work to do."

"Come back soon, Marcus," Benni said with a wave as Gray slipped his arm around her waist and waved, too.

"Will do. Tell Lilliana thank you, too. Bye." I had to hold my arm high to keep the big bag from dragging on the ground, while holding a coffee in each hand.

Once I got to the door, I looked at it and tried to figure out how I was going to get out without a problem.

But a second later, it swung toward me, and I danced backward out of the way.

"Marcus, hi," Lilliana said, pushing the door all the way to give me and my cargo room to go by.

"I'm glad you're here," I said, "I want to thank you again for doing this for me. I'm so excited for the unveiling tonight."

"Any time," she said, smiling at me with a little blush gracing her cheeks as she looked at the floor, "It was a lot of fun. And if you or the brewery need any art in the future, give me another call."

"Trust me, I will call whenever I need art." I waved the cup in my hand, and scooted outside.

Not even a full minute later, Theresa's huge truck pulled up, and I had to put the big bag in the back after I handed her the coffee.

Her eyes widened, and she grinned at her cup before she took a drink, closing her eyes with a humming sound.

"Good?" I asked, smiling at her as I shut my door.

"I love caffeine," she said, and I had to agree, even if I laughed at her in the process.

SHANE

*S*o far, so good.

The party was just getting started, the doors wide open to the night, and the temp hires doing all the actual work tonight while the employees became part of the festivities.

Yes, this was a private going away party for Van, but it was also for all of them, their family and friends, to have a chance to enjoy the last night they had with her.

It was also my chance for a possible beginning instead of just an end. I couldn't help checking the doors every few seconds looking for the one face I wanted to see more than any other.

"Don't worry," Zeda said, standing at my shoulder, appearing from somewhere in the crowd. "He'll be here."

"How can you be so sure?" I asked, taking a drink of my beer so I wouldn't keep talking, afraid that if I did, she would lay into me again like she and Van did earlier.

"Let's just say that I know some things you don't. Call it woman's intuition." She smiled at me and walked away. The bodies in the room swallowed her up as she went, blocking her from view.

She knew things I didn't?

What did that mean?

Had she heard from Marcus?

I looked back to the doors, and in the direction Zeda disappeared to.

For now, watching the doors wasn't going to give me anything except maybe an ulcer, but finding Zeda might give me a real clue.

Taking off after her, I had to smile and pretend to glad-hand my way through the throng.

Every time I thought I found her, spotted her hair or her face among all the others in the room, she would be gone again.

"Did Zeda come through here?" I asked Tyler as I passed him.

"Oh, yeah, Boss. She is probably getting ready for the announcements." He grinned. It took me a minute to even remember what he was talking about.

After everything we did here to prepare for the party and to use it to launch the competition, it all fled from my brain in the face of my worry over what the night would mean for Marcus and me.

"Thanks, Tyler," I said, patting him on the shoulder, and heading toward the stage we had set up on one end of the tasting room.

For now, a band played on the stage, although most of their songs were just background music for the moment. I wasn't sure if it would remain that way, or if, at some point in the night, people would begin dancing.

The plan was to make the announcements about the contest from the stage.

Once I reached the stage area, I didn't find any sign of Zeda.

All I saw was the lineup of the large canvases that held the designs for each brew that waited to be shown off.

Just looking at them, at everything that already came from

Marcus' idea, I wanted him here even more than before. It turned into a physical ache.

He made this happen. The buzz in the air of so many employees bragging to all their friends, families, co-workers, and customers about the contest, and how excited they were to try their own brews was all because of him.

I looked all the way across the sea of people and toward the doors again.

But it wasn't Marcus' face that I saw walk in. It was Ceecee and her friends, including at least half the big football guys from his first night at work.

Checking every last one of them as they filed inside, I looked for him anxiously.

His friends scanned the room and the people in it as they came in, but I didn't find his face.

Something inside me cracked.

No matter what he might have said to Zeda, or what she might have thought she knew, he wasn't coming.

Maybe Ceecee and the others were here to see his brew announced and report back. Maybe they were here to tell me in person that he was gone forever and why.

But they didn't need to tell me all the reasons he had. I knew them already.

And if they were here about the contest, I didn't have anything to do with that.

Van and I would see each other again. She was my cousin. This wasn't a going away party for *me* to say goodbye, which meant I didn't need to be here.

Wandering toward my office, I sidestepped people who were laughing and talking, connecting to the others around them in a way I didn't think I was able to anymore.

Just like that, the answer to the problem with buying out Van came to me.

I would sell the business.

Once, this place was my whole life. But that was when I was hanging onto the echo of the life I left behind.

Now, it would just be a terrible reminder of everything I lost.

Terrible and beautiful. That's what this place was, just like love.

A feeling as impermanent as the wind, but as powerful as a tornado was what I built this place on. It was how I dreamt this place into existence, and what fueled me through all the work that I poured into it since then.

But that cooling and refreshing wind, the one that kept pushing me on in all my pursuits for so many years had changed, shifted, and it was blowing somewhere else now.

I should have been happy for him.

Years of telling myself I would be happy for him didn't prepare me for the moment it became real, though.

Well, it was real now.

He wasn't coming.

It was all over.

For real this time.

Marcus left me, and there wasn't a damn thing I could do about it.

A mirthless laugh broke out of me as I stepped around the temps working behind the bar, flitting in and out of the kitchen with the platters of appetizers.

Some people would probably say that it was a bitter kind of justice.

Van and Zeda asked me if I would fight for him if I needed to, and I thought I had.

Looking out at the tasting room one more time before I locked myself in my office, I saw the last-minute additions of the sunflowers all over the room.

I saw the white and yellow ribbons that hung from the light fixtures and adorned the stage. I took in all the ways I made sure this space was ready for my own personal Sun to walk into it and see it for what it was. An ode to him.

But none of it mattered now.

He wasn't coming.

Grabbing the doorknob, my grip too tight, I yanked the door open and looked in my waiting, empty office.

They told me to fight.

No matter what he decided, they told me to not just accept that it was all over, to fight for him.

Staring into my office, the images of the tasting room dressed for him popped into my mind. I realized that they asked me to fight, but I decorated…

If he wasn't coming, if he wasn't going to see any of what I did, there was only one thing I could still do.

Grabbing his file from my desk, and pulling up the directions on my phone, I set my spine one last time.

Marcus wasn't coming, so I would go to him.

"Okay," I said to the empty room, forcing back all the crushing weight of the pain I feared waited to fall over me one more time, "this is me fighting."

MARCUS

*M*aneuvering the large bag containing my artwork through the bustling kitchen full of temporary staff proved more difficult than I thought.

Sending my friends in through the front doors while I brought this in through the kitchen sounded like a good idea at the time.

But I had a hard time imagining the tasting room was as much of an obstacle course as the kitchen was at the moment.

Apologizing as I slipped past even more people, forcing all of us to be more careful not to drop our burdens or trip over each other, I finally made it to the doors.

One of the servers crowded next to me with a tray, and nodded at my muttered apology and thanks as he pushed open the door then held it back while I made my way through.

Whatever I thought about the crowded nature of the kitchen, it was nothing compared to the bedlam of the tasting room.

No one in here was rowdy—it looked like mostly organized chaos—but the sheer number of people jammed in made me wonder what the building fire code was for capacity.

Maybe my grand idea for this party, to combine all the things, to get buzz going with our social media, wasn't as thoughtful as I believed it to be.

Skirting along the edge of the crowd, taking a few careful steps at a time to protect the artwork that was the biggest part of my plan here tonight, I tried to spot Shane in the crowd.

But there were too many people.

He had to be here somewhere.

I would just find him after I put my artwork with all the rest waiting behind the stage.

Good thing Zeda thought about where we would stash all of our pieces because I didn't think any other place was safe from the bodies in here.

"Marcus," Vanessa said, appearing from the throng at my side, bending to speak in my ear so she could be heard, "bring it over here. I'm so glad you got here before we started all the announcements. Andrew is waiting for you."

"You haven't told him anything, have you?" I asked, smiling to myself and hoping he would understand.

"No, of course not." She grinned and jostled my arm as she almost jumped up and down in her excitement. "This is just too good."

"I hope so," I said, tightening my grip on the art in my hand.

She led me to the stack of pieces already arranged in order of their presentations.

With her help, I uncovered the art.

Tears welled up in her eyes, and she put both hands to her chest in a very Hollywood gesture that made me smile even more.

All I could hope for was that Shane would have the same reaction to it.

"Marcus," she said, helping me put it in the place it needed to be for the announcements, "he's going to cry."

"Is it weird that I hope so?" I asked, and she laughed.

"Come on," she said, looping her arm with mine, "we need to go find Zeda."

"How soon is the announcement?" I asked, looking around for Zeda just like Vanessa was.

"Soon." She didn't elaborate, or give me an exact answer. But that was enough of an answer to make my heart squeeze. I feared the hand she was holding would become grossly sweaty.

"What's going on with the decorations?" I asked, looking up at the way the ribbons on the light fixtures paired with the flowers all over the place made this brewery feel more like a wedding venue in some fairy tale.

"Do you like it?" Vanessa smiled at me as we made our way around another knot of people who cheered her as we passed.

"Love it. It's beautiful. I just don't remember anyone talking about this while we were planning."

"It was all a last-minute change from Andrew."

"But why? He didn't like the old decor plans?"

"He thought this was sunnier," she said, stopping to look back at me with a soft smile on her face.

I took in a shuddering breath, and looked up at the way the yellow and white made the lights of the fixtures seem to drip from them, bathing the whole place in fluttering light.

"Shane did this for me?" I asked, my voice low.

Even though Vanessa couldn't have heard me, she smiled and squeezed my hand, which was all the answer I needed before she looked back out to the crowd.

"There she is," Vanessa said, pointing.

Following the line of her hand, I spotted Zeda, standing with Ceecee and chatting.

"Ceecee is with her, too."

Vanessa didn't respond, just tugged me in their direction.

Zeda and Ceecee were talking as if they knew each other, but I couldn't remember ever introducing them. Maybe there were more connections to this brewery than I realized before I started working here.

That made me smile. It felt like the universe would have managed a way for me and Shane to meet again even if I didn't start working for him.

We reached the place they were all gathered, and Zeda gave me a smirk.

"Hello, Lover Boy," Zeda said, and I grinned back at her, not minding being called that in this context at all.

"Marcus," Ceecee said, shaking her head, "you look like you're going to grab him right now, and engage in some embarrassing PDA. Maybe, tone it down?"

"Leave him alone," Theresa said, rolling her eyes and smirking at Ceecee, "the poor guy has been deprived for years."

"You, too?" Vanessa asked, sharing a loaded look with Zeda.

"I don't know what that means," I said, trying not to blush.

"She means that Andrew has become a monk in your absence," Zeda said. "It's pathetic. Even when we surprised him with a date, he made no attempt at getting a second one. You ruined him."

I had to put a hand over my mouth to hold back the laugh and the tears that wanted to burst out of me that we were both pining, heartbroken fools.

"Ridiculous. So, you both handled the separation the same way," Ceecee said, shaking her head and smiling.

"Well," I said, the smile I was fighting something I could still hear in my own voice, "once you meet the love of your life…"

"Not you, too," Zeda said, her face as if she was more than done with listening to me. It only made me smile more.

"Do we really have to hear the massive pining twice in one day?" Vanessa said, but she couldn't stifle her grin.

"Twice?" I asked, finally catching up to what they were saying. Did he talk to them about me? Did he call me the love of his life, too?

My heart beat harder in my chest. Any nerves I had about what I was planning fled from my body, replaced with a desperate need for time to speed up so I could see him again, hold him again, tell him…everything.

But a second later, I got my wish, even if it wasn't the way I was expecting.

"Shane," I said, pointing at where he was racing through the space behind the bar and slipping out through the doors to the kitchen.

"Where is he going?" Zeda asked. "We need to make the announcements."

"He was crying," I said, and they all looked at me.

Vanessa and Zeda pulled out their phones, their faces grave, as they rushed toward where Shane just disappeared.

"Did he just leave?" I asked Ceecee, every bit of the sadness and nerves of before returning in full force now that I had been without them for long enough to think they wouldn't come back.

All I wanted was to see him, faster than I expected. But now I wondered if getting that wish ruined all the other ones.

SHANE

 y phone kept going off.

Van and Zeda must have figured out that I was gone.

But missing the party and the announcements was a small price to pay if this worked.

I checked the directions on my phone again, pushing the button to ignore another call, and looked at the street signs for my next turn.

There, I made the turn, and knew I needed to keep looking for the sign for the apartment building, just in case it was like Zeda's and had the stupid entrance for guests on the wrong street.

But this time, before I saw the sign for the apartments, I saw the sign for the street and made another turn.

My phone went off again, and I ignored it just like last time.

No matter what they wanted to tell me, it wouldn't keep me from this. And I didn't want to have that conversation right now.

I just needed to keep my focus on this. I needed to keep fighting so I didn't break.

Finally, I made my way through the maze of the apartment complex, checking the numbers.

And I found it.

Parking in the first open spot, not caring if it belonged to someone and I got towed, I stared up at the number on the stone wall.

Just sitting outside his apartment, knowing I was about to knock on his door, sent everything in me rioting all over again.

But I needed to do this.

I got out of the car, locking it behind me, my phone going off in my pocket, and headed up to meet my destiny.

On the way up the stairs, my phone stopped ringing, and I pulled it out to silence it completely.

There was no reason for me to even be aware of them getting angrier and angrier with me with every ring.

After everything, it came down to something as simple as this.

I stood in front of his door with nothing, no grand romantic gesture, not even flowers, just me and my empty hands, and I knocked on the door.

Knocking only took a second. Waiting for him to answer took longer.

Then longer.

And even longer.

Okay, so maybe he didn't hear me the first time.

Raising my hand, I had to take a deep breath before I knocked again.

But even after that, there was nothing.

No sound came from inside. No one answered the door. It was just me on his porch, waiting.

"Fine," I said, after far too long when I realized he wasn't here, "it's fine. I'll just wait."

When I started the night, I thought I would be at a party,

surrounded by a visual of my feelings for him, and I would get the chance to tell him, somehow get him back.

Maybe I was deluding myself then. Maybe I was deluding myself now. But even as I sat there on the steps to his front door, looking out over the least romantic view I could imagine —a cramped, asphalt parking lot—I couldn't let go of the thread of hope I still carried.

As people came through the parking lot and the minutes turned into hours, I kept hold of that thread, refusing to think of anything except when he would come home.

Because there was no other choice.

I needed to see him tonight. And I needed to believe that I would be enough.

There was a strange thing that happened while I tried not to think, while I sat waiting for so long. Eventually, my mind wandered down paths of old memories, basking in the beauty of all the good that lived in my past. All of it was with Marcus.

Finally, another car pulled into the parking lot, and parked in one of the spots in front of the building I waited at.

By this point, I assumed it was another one of Marcus' neighbors. I barely paid attention to the car, more than happy to stay in my memories.

Hanging my head, I put my face in my hands, and tried to remember the time in the summer when we lived without air conditioning just so I could pretend to be warm as the cold seeped into my bones.

"Shane?" Marcus' voice managed to break through the block of memory I built around myself.

I looked up, slowly, not entirely convinced I wasn't hallucinating.

But there he was. Marcus stood at the bottom of the stairs, his hands wrapped around each other with tight fingers.

"Marcus, you didn't come," I said, shooting to my feet and

almost falling down the stairs, my legs screaming at finally being moved.

"You left," he said, his voice cracking as he shook his head.

"Wait…" I stumbled down the stairs, hanging on the railings to keep myself upright until Marcus met me part way, grabbing onto my arms. "You came? But I didn't see you with your friends."

A wavering smile tugged at the corners of his perfect mouth, and the little strength left in my cold, stiff legs almost went out of them.

"Of course, I came. I had to bring my artwork in through the kitchen."

Just seeing him smile, even though I could barely feel my skin, made everything better.

"But why did you leave?" Marcus asked, his voice barely there.

Lifting a hand from the railing, I reached out to touch him and paused, not sure if I was allowed to anymore.

Curling my fingers back, I dropped my hand again and said, "I came here. To fight for you."

He sucked in a breath, and took another step upward, bringing his face an inch from mine.

"We fought our way back to each other," he said, his gaze soft and like a caress as he touched every bit of my face, "you don't have to fight anymore."

"Marcus," I said, putting a hand to the front of his coat, right over his heart, and leaning in, my eyes slipping shut.

He leaned toward me, his eyes closed, and for the first time in years I was going to kiss the love of my life.

A kid screamed from one of the apartments, and my eyes flew open as I leaned back, away from him to look around at what the problem was.

"No you don't," Marcus said, drawing my vision back to him, "I waited too long to let you get distracted now."

Without warning, he grabbed the front of my coat, and pressed his lips to mine.

But, after so long without feeling his kiss, I couldn't now. All I could feel was the searing heat of him.

He pulled away after only a second and his hands were on my face, his eyes wide and full of fear.

"Shane," he said, his voice louder and harder, "why are you so cold?"

"It took you a long time to come home," I said, thinking it was obvious and made perfect sense.

Marcus scoffed, muttering swear words under his breath as he turned me around, wrapping an arm around my waist, and leading me back up the stairs towards his front door.

As soon as he got me inside, the warmth of the room almost stung against my skin, but he took another moment to look at me as I marveled at him.

"I love you, Marcus," I said, not able to wait another minute before he heard me say it.

Everything about his face turned to something close to bliss as he closed his eyes and leaned into me, allowing me some of his heat.

"I love you, Shane," he said.

MARCUS

Waking up in the morning to see Shane's eyes staring at me from the other side of the bed was like my dreams had become real. For a second I feared it was like that moment when something bad happens, and I would wake up not remembering for a minute, like he wasn't actually here and I just forgot about our separation.

But this moment didn't end, and he didn't disappear.

"Are you real?" he whispered, like he was as afraid to break the spell of being back together as I was.

Lifting a hand, I touched his cheek, as warm as my palm and just as real.

"I always knew you were real, but this?" I smiled, "This can't be real. I can't be lucky enough to have this again."

"Marcus," he said in that way of his, closing his eyes and putting his hand over mine, holding it against his cheek.

He leaned forward and kissed me, his lips warm and soft, and made me feel more at home than anything in all the time I spent without him.

But only a few moments later, as his arms wrapped around me and pulled me close, my alarm went off.

Shane groaned, and I rolled over to shut it off.

"Can we just stay in bed all day?" he asked, pulling me close again.

"No," I said, kissing his nose and sitting up, pulling him with me, "as much as I wish we could, your cousin leaves today."

He sat up with me, kissing my shoulder, and gazing at me with a grin.

"Van will understand," he said, and I laughed.

"You better hurry, or I will leave you here, Shane," I said, getting out of the bed, and heading toward the bathroom.

It didn't take us long to get ready, although every time we had to move past each other, we both stopped and stared for a minute before smiling and going on with what we were doing.

But, when we climbed into his car, we were only five minutes later than we wanted to be to head to Zeda's and send Vanessa off.

Shane stretched out his hand, his fingers running along mine.

It was difficult to pay attention to the rest of the world when I could spend eternity looking at him.

Wrapping my fingers around his, holding his hand tight, never wanting to let it go again, I leaned my head back on the seat and indulged in staring.

"They all know we're coming?" he asked, still focused on the road even as he leaned further my way.

"Of course," I said, looking down at my phone where it sat in my lap.

"And they know we're coming together?" he asked, picking up my hand and kissing the back of it.

"If any of them think that, after last night, I would be away from you for any longer than I absolutely have to be for the next thirty years, then they've lost their senses."

Shane grinned, his thumb making circles along the back of my hand.

"Thirty years?" he asked. "I'm not sure if I should be upset you only plan to be with me for the next thirty years or thrilled you want me around so much."

"Oh, shush." I rolled my eyes as he chuckled. "You know that I only picked that number so that at some point before we retire and are on a fixed income, you can plan me a surprise birthday party."

At that, he burst out laughing and I smiled, reveling in watching as the joy returned to his face.

"You know," he said, his laughter dying and his face suddenly sober as he stole a glance at me before focusing on the road in front of us again, "last night I tried to put together a kind of surprise party for you."

Last night we weren't able to talk much. We held each other, he warmed up, and we kissed, a lot, before we both finally fell asleep, more at peace than either of us had been in years. But I did know what he tried to do with the party, even if we didn't hash it all out.

"Just so you know, I loved the decorations," I said, my voice low as I folded my other hand around our clasped ones. "They were beautiful, and went very well with the artwork I had made for my brew."

He looked my way, a question in his eyes, before he tore them away from me again to be safe while we drove.

"Are you going to tell me about this artwork you had done, or are you just going to keep leaving cryptic hints?"

"No. I'm not doing either. After we go to Zeda's and say goodbye to Vanessa, I'm going to show you."

Shane grinned at me, and lifted our joined hands to touch my chin with his thumb.

"You're cute when you put your nose in the air, and act high and mighty," he said.

"While you're cute all the time," I said, kissing that same thumb.

"Marcus," he said in a way that made everything in me turn to mush.

I wriggled and settled further against the seat I was in, never wanting to stop looking at him or hearing him say that to me.

"Can you say that again?" I asked, my voice low and giving away more than I thought based on the way he glanced my way, lifted a brow, and heat entered his gaze.

"Do you like it when I say your name?"

"As much as you talk about the sun, Shane, there is nothing in this world more beautiful than the way you say my name. More than anything else, I missed hearing you say that."

He looked at me then. For a long moment, his eyes weren't trained on the road as they should have been, and more was in his eyes than I expected.

Eventually, he turned back to the road with a sigh and shudder that ran through his whole body.

"The thing I missed you saying more than anything else was what you told me last night."

"You were a fool for letting yourself get too cold?"

"Very funny. No." His eyes met mine again and his look said my name. "That you love me."

He focused again on what he was doing, and I took a deep breath, preparing to tell him every day for the rest of our lives.

"All this time, all these years," I said, "when I looked for you, when I believed you didn't want me to find you, when I tried to be furious with you, when I thought I would never see you again, all this time I loved you. And I love you now."

Shane leaned further over, stretching into my seat, his eyes darting my way, and his lips searching.

Just like last night, I leaned in and placed a kiss on his lips. But now I trailed kisses down his neck as he returned to his own seat again.

"Marcus," he said, this time my name didn't come out as an I love you. This time it was a warning.

But I just made a hmmm noise against his neck, and waited for him to pull away from me.

He didn't.

A thrill went through me as I realized, he might not be willing to tell me no again.

I could get used to this.

"It's a good thing Van is my cousin and loves me," I said as Marcus followed me into the brewery, our hands still linked together.

She handled it well, really. But she was so mad at me that it was a close thing.

The reality was, I didn't think it was the fact she was family that saved me from her wrath for leaving in the middle of her going away party and silencing my phone.

Looking back at the grin on Marcus' face, at the light shining out of him, I was pretty sure she only forgave me because she knew how much he meant to me.

"Otherwise, she might have tied you to the side of a bus leaving town, and told you to hope for the best," Marcus said making me laugh.

But the noise that filtered through into the kitchen from the tasting room killed the laughter in my throat.

"No one is supposed to be here," I muttered, stopping in my tracks and tucking Marcus behind me. Were we being robbed?

"Well, then, they have some explaining to do," Marcus said,

darting around me, letting go of my hand and managing to get past my grasping for him.

"Marcus," I said, my voice a low hiss as I hurried after him. I tried to grab him back, and wanted to run with him as far from whoever was here that shouldn't have been as we could.

But when I made it through the doors to the tasting room, I slammed into Marcus' back.

"Oof," I said, grabbing his shoulders to steady myself, I looked around him at whatever had struck him so much he was stone still and didn't even react to me running into him.

"What is this?" I asked out loud, although I knew Marcus didn't have a clue what was going on either.

Zeda looked up from the back of the room. She was standing behind multiple tables with a notebook in her hand.

The tables in front of her had other employees sitting on one side, and customers on the other as they filled out paperwork and spoke with the customers.

Everyone went about their business, as if Marcus and I were the only ones here who had no idea what was going on.

Another person answered the phone when it rang while they sat at another table and filled out paperwork, too.

I stepped around Marcus and stood next to him, trying to figure out what we were missing.

"Did you plan something?" I asked him. Maybe he did know and just forgot?

"No," he said, shaking his head and taking my hand. "I didn't know we had anything going on today.

Zeda tapped all the crew members at the tables on their shoulders, and spoke in each one's ear before she closed her notebook and making her way over to us.

"Can you explain this to me?" I asked her, still watching as one of the customers at the tables seem to finish what they were doing, shook hands with the person speaking with them, and walked away. The crew member shuffled their papers and made notes as if they were waiting for another customer.

"We were getting too many calls," Zeda said, as if that answered my question at all.

"I don't know what that means," I said.

"Marcus' plan for the party last night seems to have had some unintended consequences," she said.

"But…" Marcus muttered, looking up at Zeda and then at me before turning his bewildered gaze back to her, "are they good consequences, or bad?"

Good question. Trying to count the number of people here, I tried not to panic that we had somehow made this many people irate for some reason.

"Well," Zeda said, handing over her notebook, open to a page with a column of figures that were totaled at the bottom and equaled a huge sum.

"Z," I said, rubbing my free hand over my face and shaking my head, none of what she was pointing out made any sense to me so far.

Marcus looked at the notebook, his eyebrows high, and looked up at me.

All I could do was shrug. It didn't enlighten me as to what was going on either.

He turned back to her, holding my hand tighter.

"Please," Marcus said, his voice flat, and not sounding like he was begging at all. He sounded more like he was trying to hold in his exasperation, "You're going to have to spell it out for us. Because we still don't understand what those figures mean, or what everyone is doing here."

Zeda sighed, then pulled her notebook back to her chest.

"The party last night made a bunch of people interested in doing business with us," Zeda said, looking over her shoulder toward the tables. "Mostly event planners. We are taking their orders for their special events, crafting contracts for supplying some event spaces, and even trying to navigate the few that want to rent out the tasting room for things like weddings."

"Really?" I asked, leaning around her to look at the crew members and customers, I watched another couple walked in the door.

"If you stayed last night," Zeda said and I cringed, "you would know that it went better than anyone expected."

Marcus grinned up at me, and I let go of his hand to slip my arms around him.

"You made this happen," I said, looking into the eyes of the man I loved more than I could ever express to him fully.

"But how?" he asked, eyes wide.

"This place had one of the best parties of the year last night," Zeda said, turning away from us to look out over the people waiting, "and nothing went wrong all night."

She looked over her shoulder at us as she started back toward her post behind the tables, "Apparently that's a big deal."

"Do you think this will help?" Marcus asked, looking at me and tightening his hold on my waist.

"Not only do those figures look like this will help, but, I think between this and the other things we're doing, including the rest of the contest, we'll be able to take care of Van. At least a big payment to start." I leaned toward him, so thankful I could do this again. But he pulled away before I was able to kiss him.

When I looked at him, confused, he grinned and grabbed my hand, tugging me after him.

"Speaking of the competition," he said, walking backward and pulling me along with him. His eyes darted to where all the artwork was still resting along the back wall behind the stage, "you still haven't heard about my brew yet."

"Marcus," I said, slow and careful. I smiled, but the glint in his eye said he was up to something.

We made our way to the art, and it only took me a second to

figure out which one was his. I sucked in a breath, awed by his own grand, romantic gesture.

The artwork was in yellows and golds. The name of the brew was Sunny Dream, but, hidden among the bottom of the sunbeams, as if they were shining out them or into them and the viewer couldn't tell the difference, were two figures.

Nothing about the figures would have been enough to tip off anyone else, but I recognized the height difference that made the one with Marcus' coloring just a bit shorter than the one with my coloring.

I recognized us in the figures laying next to each other, holding hands, on the bottom of this gorgeous piece.

But it was the name, him owning Sunny, and calling this his dream that made it as clear as he was in front of me.

"You…" I choked back the tears that threatened at the back of my eyes, pulling him to me, and burying my head in the crook of his neck. "You made yours for me."

"Of course, I did," he said, running his hands along my back. "Everything I do is for you."

"Zeda," I called, pushing the button on the intercom to her experiment room from my office, trying not to whine.

"Yes, Boss Babe?" she said back over the intercom.

"Nope. Don't like that nickname, either." I ran my hands through my hair, and tried not be snappy when I was so tired and had yet to get my coffee.

"Wow," she said, "you sound crabby."

"Too tired."

"Do I need to tell the boss to stop with the elaborate dates?"

"Please," I said. Well, more like whined.

"Sorry, Boss Boyfriend. No can do."

"You sound way too happy to turn me down."

"I am," she said, a smugness to her tone that even the intercom couldn't get rid of.

"Zeda." Yep. I was definitely whining.

"After everything he put me through with all the pining and tears and nonsense, this obsession he has with overly-complicated dates that leave you a mess the next day is payback. Personally. For me."

There were no other words for me to say, so I just groaned.

"Mini Boss, do you not like the dates?" she asked, her voice quieter.

"Of course, I like them. I love them. But I would love anything I did with him, even if all we did was stay home and talk about nothing. I love him and want *him*, Zeda. Not overly-complicated dates that just leave me tired, and in need of coffee."

"Good answer. Okay, I'll talk to him."

"Thank you," I said, letting out a long breath and resting my forehead on my desk, squeezing my eyes closed.

"Boss Boytoy?" she asked.

"Yuck. Not that one either, or Mini Boss. Ew."

"Fine," she said, laughing through the intercom. "But why did you call me again?"

"Oh," I said, rubbing my eyes and sitting up, trying to focus on my job and the thing I wanted to get out of the way first thing this morning because I thought it would be easy. "I need to do the final test on my brew. Is it ready?"

"Yep. I'll get that set up."

"Thanks, Zeda."

"No problem, Boss Boyfriend."

She disconnected before I could add that to the list of nick-names I didn't like.

"Why do you look unhappy to be called the boss' boyfriend exactly?" Shane asked, laughter in his voice as he came into my office, and put a coffee from The Big O on my desk.

"I love you," I said, looking up at him from my seat as he grinned and leaned over me to give me a quick kiss.

"Love you, too, Sunny. Now tell me why you make a face at Boss Boyfriend?" he asked, leaning back to sit on my desk and give me that soft smile I loved so much.

"Because I prefer my name." I took a drink of the coffee, and relished in the first moment the caffeine hit my tongue before getting back to the point I was making. "Plus, as much as I love being the boss' boyfriend, when she calls me that, it makes me feel like some gold digger."

I shuddered but Shane dropped down, crouching next to my chair, and wrapped me in his arms even as he grinned.

"That would only be true if you weren't the one who basically bailed me out with all your hard work and brilliant ideas." He leaned in and kissed me, the feel of his lips on mine all these weeks later still enough to make me forget the world.

Since we were at work, like so many times before, he was still responsible. He pulled back to look at me, and straightening my hair where I must have messed it up by running my hands through it.

"Do you know how much I love you?" I asked.

"As much as I love you, Marcus," he said, his voice caressing my name and turning it into a way to say he loved me twice.

Work or not, I leaned in and kissed him again. I had years of missed kisses to make up for.

AFTERWORD

Thank you for reading!

If you enjoyed this book, please leave a review at your favorite bookseller.

Don't forget to go to darleneeverly.com and sign up for the newsletter to be the first to know when the next Comfort Food romance makes it to the table.

The next book in the series, Favorite Beans will be coming in February 2023 and the first two books in the series, Personal Pan and Cupcake Queens are available now!

ACKNOWLEDGMENTS

A whole hearted thank you to Bean, the Rottens, and all of my friends and family. A big bag of thanks to Jupiter Alley and Krystal and Lucy for their help in making this happen, as well as the team at Wishing Well. Sometimes, a drink is exactly what you want it to be at exactly the right moment.

ALSO BY DARLENE EVERLY

Personal Pan

Cupcake Queens

Until We Didn't

www.ingramcontent.com/pod-product-compliance
Lightning Source LLC
Chambersburg PA
CBHW030630190726
48286CB00008B/2464